DREAMING OF HER BEST FRIEND'S KISS

Cowboy Mountain Christmas
Book 5

JESSIE GUSSMAN

Contents

Acknowledgments

Cover art by Lara Wynter
Editing by Heather Hayden
Narration by Jay Dyess
Author Services by CE Author Assistant

Listen to the unabridged audio for FREE performed by Jay Dyess on the Say with Jay channel on YouTube. Get early access to all of Jay's recordings and listen to Jessie's books before they're available to the general public, plus get daily Bible readings by Jay and bonus scenes by becoming a Say with Jay channel member.

Prologue

"Everyone can see the two of them are perfect together," Race Steiner said, taking a bite of the pizza.

"Everyone but themselves," his wife, Penny, gently corrected, her brows lifted in that way she had that made him want to smile and kiss her at the same time.

"You're right as usual."

Pizza wasn't their normal choice of meal with Penny being a former midwife and him a former cardiac surgeon.

Both of them knew what pizza did to the body.

However, he'd lost their bet, and that meant he owed her a pizza.

He tried to bite back a grin as he chewed on the cheesy deliciousness. He was working on getting himself into another bet. A friendly wager between a husband and wife about their children.

Only to help them, of course.

Typically, his wife won.

Which was just fine by him.

He liked pizza.

"The problem is you can't just go up and tell her that she needs to fall in love with her best friend."

"No. Definitely not." His wife tilted her head. "You've learned something over the years."

He grinned, enjoying her teasing. She knew him like no one else. "I have to give all the credit to you. At least in emotional matters of the heart anyway."

"Of course. There's nothing I can tell you about physical hearts that you don't already know."

"Emotional hearts are more complicated by far," he said with sincerity.

His wife set her pizza down, picked up her napkin, and dabbed at the sides of her mouth with a thoughtful look on her face. "It's just, everything you tell Blakely to do, she always wants to do the opposite. She's completely selfless and was always obedient and tried with a good attitude to do what we wanted, but she has this unconscious rebellion that if she knows it's what she's expected to do, she wants to do something else."

"Yeah. She's not rebellious, but it's like she hears 'can't' and sees it as a challenge."

"And hears 'can' and views it as boring."

They nodded together, their words not effective in explaining, exactly, what it was about their daughter Blakely.

Neither one of them viewed her as anything but wonderful, but she definitely always rose to the challenge, and when there wasn't a challenge, she created her own.

Penny picked up her pizza. "That's probably why she's become such a great trick rider. Most people, after they'd fallen off and broken two arms and a leg at various times, would have given up and found something slightly easier to do."

"Not Blakely. She's just as determined now as she ever was to make a living doing trick riding." Race checked the time on his watch. "Have you heard from her?" Blakely was trying out for a spot on the top traveling western show in the country.

He wished his daughter the best, and he truly did hope that she got the job, even though it was a traveling show that would take her from city to city for the next year and a half.

He hated to lose her for that long.

And he wasn't entirely sure that was the best thing for her.

But she hadn't asked for his opinion, and typically, unless there was something pressing, he tried to keep his opinion to himself until it was asked for.

Most of the time, he was successful.

"I'm sorry. I did. While you were taking a shower, she called. She's settled into her hotel room, and she's on the schedule to perform tomorrow morning at nine o'clock. I told her we'd pray for her." Penny paused with the pizza halfway to her mouth. "I didn't tell her that we would pray that she got the position." Her face was serious.

"It just doesn't sit right. Doesn't feel like that's what she's supposed to do. Did she say she's prayed about this?"

"No. I think she knows it's not really what the Lord wants for her life, but it's what she wants. And she's going after it with everything she has. Like she's always done."

Race nodded thoughtfully, his eyes on the pizza box. Part of his mind was rolling over in his head whether or not he should have another piece, and part of his mind was on his daughter, who never did things halfway but jumped in with her whole heart and soul.

It made for some really hard landings.

Lord, work this out according to your plan. Please keep her safe and close to you.

A bullet prayer. He prayed them all the time. Especially for his children. But also for the members of his church. Daily, minute by minute, people would roll through his mind, and he'd lift them up before the Lord. It was part of his job as pastor.

"Martin is out on the rodeo circuit anyway. Maybe we are the ones that are wrong, and their separate directions really are God's plan for their lives."

"Maybe." He definitely wasn't convinced of it.

"Well, unless God brings something to your mind, I'm fresh out of ideas. Although," she said, pausing to take a sip of her water, "our plans worked out beautifully with Ethan, and with Denver, and you really had a great plan with Crew and Burgundy. That Santa thing worked out better than I ever thought it would."

"Yeah. It was kind of hard for me to have the whole Santa thing in church, but it's the idea of giving, and Burgundy and Crew definitely benefited, as well as a bunch of other people in the church." He sighed. "Blakely and Martin took it over for a while, but it just didn't work out as well."

"They were already friends. They need a different kind of push," she said thoughtfully. "You know you did a good job with West too."

"Everyone could see that Poppy was perfect for him. He needed her."

"And man wasn't made to be alone," Penny said, a sentence both of them believed in strongly. The Bible was clear about that.

Race felt strongly that if God had taken the time to write them a handbook and give it to them, they should read it, study it, and use it to guide their lives.

Since God was quite capable of writing a book that was applicable down through the ages, being that He was God and He created the universe, Race always felt it was silly for anyone to pick and choose what he would and would not believe out of it.

It was an awful lot like the created telling the Creator he knew better than the Creator did.

Race figured after he created his first universe and a few planets, and maybe a person or two, then he would be qualified to start telling God what was best for him. Until that happened, he'd follow The Book.

He made a decision, picking up another piece of pizza from the box. They only splurged once in a while, and having another piece wasn't going to hurt anything. He watched as cheese strung out, thinning, as he lifted the slice and set it on his plate.

"Dante is coming to Mistletoe. He was gonna spend a month here anyway."

"But..." Penny looked at him, her brows drawn down in confusion. Blakely wasn't the girl that Dante was coming for. Dante didn't know that. And neither did the girl.

"No. I'm not thinking a match between Blakely and Dante. Goodness, that would never work. Even I can see that. But..."

It only took a second or two for his wife's eyes to widen and understanding to dawn across her face. "A decoy?"

"Exactly."

His wife nodded, smiling. "You're brilliant." She lifted her pizza and held it in front of her mouth. "Probably smart enough to be a brain surgeon."

He laughed. "I think I'll stick with hearts."

"You're definitely getting better."

Chapter One

Blakely Barclay sat behind the wheel of her pickup, driving in the right lane just barely over the minimum speed limit for the interstate, her hands on the wheel, her mind a million miles away.

Her heart felt sick, her chest ached, and she'd spent the last two hundred miles biting back tears.

Her horses, Candy and Kisses, were in the back of the trailer.

Whimsically, she imagined they were feeling just as dejected as she was.

It wasn't their fault she was driving home in defeat. They had performed perfectly.

She was the one who hadn't.

She could almost forgive herself, if she had messed up something difficult. Like jumping through hoops of fire or riding backward standing up, one foot on each horse's back.

But it hadn't been that.

She hadn't checked her foot knot in her trick riding saddle, and one of the easiest tricks in the book—the one where she hung by one foot upside down as her horse galloped around the ring—had turned into a near catastrophe as the knot came loose, her foot slipped out, and she landed facedown in the dirt.

She hadn't even bothered to change her clothes.

She still had sawdust in her hair.

She didn't give a flip.

She'd trained for years to make a living doing something she loved, and she hadn't even gotten into the final ten.

After she'd fallen, she might as well have packed her horses up and started home then, but she'd finished her routine—everything required in the tryout. And she'd performed it all beautifully. If without heart.

Because she knew performing beautifully wasn't going to be enough after she'd landed in the dirt.

Turning her turn signal on, she pulled over into the exit lane, figuring to stop at the rest stop to check her horses and grab a coffee.

Maybe that would pick her up.

Her eyelids weren't falling closed, but she was having trouble concentrating. She just wanted to curl up in a ball somewhere and cry for really long time.

She definitely didn't want to go home and face her parents and her friends and everyone in the town of Mistletoe who'd known what she was doing and where she was going and had the faith that she would be successful.

She was coming back a failure, and she hated that.

Her phone rang as she pulled into a long parking slot between two big rigs, and she answered it, slouching in her seat, knowing this was probably the one person in the world who could understand how she was truly feeling.

"Hey, Martin."

"Wow. That bad?"

Her lips quivered, half trying to cry, half trying to smile, that he would know just from her tone that she had screwed up.

"Yeah. My knot was loose, and I fell off Kisses while I was hanging from one foot. I did everything else, but...there's no way."

She couldn't keep her tone upbeat. She was barely beating the tears back.

"Bummer. Did you check your knot?"

"No." She hated even admitting it.

"Why not, Whiplash?" he asked, using the nickname he'd given her years ago when she'd fallen off a horse that had stopped and she hadn't. He probably knew it would make her smile.

"Why didn't I? Because I'm stupid."

"Sorry, Whip. Got to agree with you on that one."

"Thanks, Staples," she said, almost able to hear his lips turning up at his own nickname, which he'd gotten honestly—by stapling his finger into a fence post, not realizing what he'd done until he'd gotten two staples in, hence the plural. It had been a beast getting the staples out. It still made her cringe, but it had been ten years and they could laugh about it now. "You're a great friend."

She closed her eyes, the smile fading from her mouth, and propped an elbow on her steering wheel, putting her head down on her hand. "I'm fine, by the way. Thanks for asking."

"I didn't figure you were in the hospital. Although, after a flub like that, you'd probably drive home with a broken leg just because you were so mad at yourself."

Yeah. He was so right. Martin knew her better than anyone. Right now, that felt good.

"I'm sorry, I know things aren't really going any better for you. Are you ready for tomorrow?"

"As ready as I'll ever be. But this is it for me. If I don't place well enough to make it to the semifinals, I've got to come home. I'm running out of money, and I have a ranch to run."

"I'll be home. I can do it."

"Two people wouldn't be enough. I'm not gonna dump it all on one."

"You know I'll hold things together as well as I can so you can stay out on the circuit."

"I know. I've just been thinking it might be time for me to hang up my dream. I've been chasing the rodeo bareback title for years. And I get close...then nothing. Bad draws, bad timing, bad luck, or stupidity on my part. I've just been thinking lately that everything seems to be going wrong this year. Even worse than last. And maybe this just isn't what I'm meant to do."

"Martin. I can't believe you're talking like that. You've always said you were going to chase this dream until you caught it. You can't quit."

"Hey, you're driving home. I might as well drive home too."

"I'm driving home because there is no more chasing my dream. I didn't make it. There isn't another rodeo somewhere else for me tomorrow."

"I know. I just...just am tired of fighting."

"If you want it, you have to work for it. It's not going to come easy." He already knew that, but she couldn't even imagine Martin not going after the title. He always spent his summers running the rodeo circuit and doing fairly well. He even had a fan following and was a favorite on local TV.

Of course, the bull riders were the big draw, with national recognition, but the bareback guys had their own fan club, albeit smaller.

"I know." His words were half annoyed, half appreciative, knowing she spoke as someone who always had his best interest at heart.

But she understood his frustration. When a person felt like everything was against him, having someone tell him he just needed to work harder and be persistent didn't really make him feel better.

She wouldn't appreciate that right now. But they were in different situations, because there was no next tryout for her. This was the one she had needed to ace.

"How are Candy and Kisses taking it?" Martin asked.

Again, the guy just knew her. She supposed, being that they had been inseparable since she had moved to Mistletoe after Race and

Penny had adopted her, it made sense. They had more than ten years of pretty much hanging out in each other's pockets.

There wasn't another person she loved or trusted more in the world than Martin.

"They're taking it pretty hard too," she said. "I just got off at the rest stop, was going to go back and check on them, make sure they're doing okay. I'm sure they can't wait to get home and mope around."

Just like her. She didn't even want to ride. It was pretty bad when she didn't want to ride.

"Well, I might be there the day after tomorrow, if things don't go well tomorrow."

It hit Blakely then, that because she hadn't made it, wasn't going to be touring the country as a trick rider, she was free.

"I have to take the horses home, and I'll check things around the ranch, make sure your hire guy's doing everything he's supposed to. Then I can come see you. You're in Oklahoma tomorrow, right?"

"It's a pretty long drive. You don't have to do that."

"I'd like to. I always love watching you. And maybe give you a little buzz just knowing there is someone in the stands not just rooting for you..." She thought about all of the fans he already had. Mostly women. Girls. "But someone who knows you and loves you and believes in you, because you are the best."

Despite her own disappointments, she smiled at that. She could almost hear her dad saying the best way to get out of your funk was to put your focus on someone else and start helping them.

Her dad was always right. Sometimes, she didn't like to admit it; sometimes, she liked to challenge what he said and test to make sure he was. She didn't like to take things at face value.

"You know I'd love to have you. I'd really love it if you were here. But you'd have to drive all day today and then hop in your truck and drive most of the day tomorrow. It's not worth it."

"It is for me. What else am I going to do?"

"Get a real job?" he said, with only a little bit of sarcasm in his voice.

She didn't rise to the bait. She gave horseback riding lessons and stabled horses on Martin's farm, which made her enough to make rent and be happy. In return for using his facilities, she was basically his free hired hand. They didn't keep track of who owed who what.

Taking a deep breath, she felt the weight on her chest lifting and realized she was already starting to bounce back. Talking to her best friend was the best therapy available.

Probably tonight when she put her head on the pillow and didn't have anything else to think about, she might get down again. She probably would shed a few tears.

But not now. Now she was excited about supporting a friend. He would have been there for her if he hadn't been on the circuit. She could do the same for him.

"If it makes you feel better, you can just assume I'm not coming, but I'll be there. That's what friends are for."

"You've definitely been a good friend. Thanks."

"You've been the same for me. It's the least I can do. I'll be in the stands, pulling for you all the way."

Chapter Two

Martin pulled his rope tight and settled carefully down on the bronc's back.

Blakely had come just like she promised, but her presence hadn't helped him in the saddle bronc riding.

But bareback was always his thing, and while he made it a point to never mingle with fans, ever, not even after he was done riding, he and Blakely had met in the back, and her unbridled enthusiasm and deep devotion and support and belief in him had bolstered his spirits.

He hated being so down. Normally, he was pretty easygoing and just rolled with the punches. They both did. Maybe that's why they got along so well together. They were really great at encouraging each other. Like Blakely had just done for him.

Obviously, his negative attitude was only going to produce negative results.

He needed to stay positive and believe this was going to be his best ride.

Forcing his mind to shut down, to focus only on the ride in front of him, he went through what he knew about the horse, Trucker Boy

—he jumped out of the gate, took two crow hops, and started bucking high. Most likely he'd veer right, finishing strong and high.

As soon as Martin had known which bronc he drew, he'd watched some videos on it. The horse was pretty predictable.

Tightening the rope, he jerked his head at his good friend Ty, and the gate flew open.

The first two crow hops were exactly what he expected, and he leaned back, pulling on the rope and getting his legs up, spurs in.

Perfect position, and he intrinsically felt this would be a high-scoring ride.

Every video Martin had watched, Trucker Boy had done the exact same thing.

Figures, this was the ride he tried something new.

Martin had been so sure he knew what Trucker Boy was going to do that his body was already positioning himself for the straight, high bucks when Trucker Boy went left.

He hadn't been expecting that, of course.

Trucker Boy wasn't even bucking crazy, and even if he were, it was almost unheard of for Martin to fall off a bareback ride.

Maybe not get a great points ride, that happened, but to fall?

Hardly ever.

But he just couldn't right himself, couldn't get his balance, and once Trucker Boy felt Martin off center, he seemed to put even more effort into getting the cowboy off his back.

Martin couldn't blame him. When victory was close, a person—or a horse—had a tendency to go after it with even more than he ever thought he had.

He fought to stay on. It would be a low-point ride, but at least it would be points.

He just couldn't.

Every time he hit the ground, it seemed to get harder. This was no exception. It jarred the shoulder he dislocated on his last ride last fall, then the rest of his body hit dirt and he struck his hip bone, pain shooting down his leg and up his right side.

A hot shower would feel good tonight. He rolled, automatically searching for where the horse was, making sure his body would stay out from underneath the sharp hooves, but Trucker Boy wasn't interested in chasing him nor in grinding him into the dirt.

That was one of the many nice things about riding broncs rather than the bulls. Typically, once a person was off, they weren't the slightest bit interested in him. If he could keep from getting stepped on and keep from breaking anything on the landing, he was home free.

Nothing was broken, but he felt about as dejected as he'd ever felt in his life before.

Stupid mistake. Why couldn't he stop making stupid mistakes?

Maybe this isn't the plan God has for your life.

Shut up. Just shut up.

Maybe it wasn't normal to talk to himself, but he was sick of that voice in his head telling him what he was doing wasn't what he should be doing.

Of course it was. This is what he'd trained for all his life.

He didn't want to do anything else.

Maybe it's not about what you want. Maybe you need to think about what God wants.

Shut up.

Brushing his chaps off, he took a couple swipes at his butt and gathered his rope.

At the very least, he and Blakely could commiserate together. Maybe they could conspire to blow something up.

"THANK GOD FOR MODERN TRANSPORTATION, RIGHT?" Blakely said, low and slightly pinched, with her cheek pressed against her gun barrel, sighting down it before she gently and carefully squeezed the trigger.

The pumpkin, sitting fifty yards away, exploded with a satisfying burst of flying orange flesh.

She grinned. It was an easy shot, and they both knew it. But he probably enjoyed seeing the flying squash flesh just as much as she.

"Modern transportation that provides us pumpkins in June, so we can shoot them and do something with the pent-up frustration that comes from a spectacular failure?" Martin asked, with humor in his voice, yes, but disappointment laced there deeply as well.

The bitterness of defeat still hadn't had time to seep out. Not for either of them.

Maybe it never would.

But it had only been a day since he'd fallen off Trucker Boy and packed his stuff up, leaving the rodeo circuit and the friends he'd spent every summer with for the last decade and more behind as he went back to his ranch.

They'd worked their fingers to the bone today, fixing fence, digging holes, and hauling heavy, twelve-foot gates to the back pasture. Jobs that had needed to be done for a while and the perfect jobs for two people who were frustrated and upset.

Their minds might not stop, but their bodies were exhausted.

Not too exhausted to do some target shooting.

"Remind me to thank your mother for grabbing these pumpkins at the store," she said to Martin as she worked the lever and sighted down her shotgun barrel again. Even her aching shoulder from the recoil of her 20 gauge wasn't enough to make her want to stop.

"I guess she's been around us long enough to know what it takes to bring both of us out of a funk."

"Guns and squash?" She lifted her cheek from the gun barrel and gave him a sideways look. "I'm not sure what that says about us. Probably nothing good."

"I don't care. Blow the thing up. It's making me feel better."

She laughed with him, then took a moment to sight down the barrel before she squeezed off another shot.

"Pretty sure that one's ready for the pie plate. Your turn. I'll go set a few up for you."

Martin was a better shot than she was, and he had a more powerful gun. It didn't take him long to demolish his pumpkins as well.

"So, you're really done on the circuit?" she asked as he straightened back up, popping the used casing out of his gun and gripping it in his arm, barrel down, as he faced her.

"I've had this voice in my head for a while. I haven't said anything because I don't want to listen to it. You're the only person I'm gonna say anything to about it."

Blakely nodded. That wasn't unusual. She never really put terms on their relationship, other than best friends. Which was a little odd, considering that she had two great sisters and he had three brothers he was really close to as well. But somehow, they just clicked with each other. It wasn't uncommon at all for them to tell each other things that no one else knew.

"I know what you're going to say, and I think you should listen to it," she said, keeping her face serious and her voice low.

"You do? You've been hearing the same voice?"

She nodded. "I have."

His eyes narrowed just slightly. After all, he did know her, and he probably figured she could be messing with him. She kept her face standing-beside-the-casket serious as his eyes swept over her.

Finally, with a little suspicion, he said, "What is your voice saying?"

"It's saying, 'Let Martin go. He needs to fulfill his destiny as an underwear model in New York City.'"

He huffed out a laugh, shoving her shoulder, making her lose her balance. She took two steps to the side, laughing.

"I'm sorry. I just couldn't help myself. You have like seventeen girls that were hanging on the fence screaming your name while you were riding. And it wasn't even that big of a rodeo. It's embarrassing."

"Tell me about it." He rolled his eyes, rubbing the back of his neck.

"You like it."

He shook his head. "It's nice to know that there are people who love what I do, but having a bunch of women that I don't even know screaming my name and acting like my personality is better than what it actually is doesn't do anything for me. You know that."

He set his gun down on the back of the four-wheeler, the muscles under his t-shirt rippling as he did so, and Blakely's eyes caught on them.

Normally, Martin was just Martin, and she didn't pay too much attention to how he looked.

But for some reason, his shoulders caught her eye today, along with the muscles under his shirt.

Maybe it was her mentioning the underwear model. Not that she gave a flip about any underwear models. She didn't have any use for some dude with oiled-up muscles who didn't know how to use them except in the gym. Lots of girls loved guys like that, and good for them, but it seemed worthless to her.

She didn't want some guy she could work circles around.

She wanted someone more like Martin. Someone who knew his way around the farm, who had skills that were practical and useful, who had a great sense of humor, and he was sensitive without being girly.

Yeah, she wasn't going to settle for anything less. She knew there were guys out there like that, because Martin was one.

Bella, his cattle dog mix, lifted her head from where she was lying in the shade under the four-wheeler. When Martin made no move to leave, she laid her head back down, her ears perked but her eyes closed.

Like most dogs, she didn't enjoy shooting, but she wasn't scared of their guns.

"I guess I kinda know what you're saying. It's nice to have fans, but even though they're gorgeous and available, and they want you,

you'd rather be here on the ranch, with your best friend, shooting instead."

Martin snorted. "You keep acting like that, and I'll have to rethink my decision."

"You love me and you know it." She bumped his shoulder with hers and laid her gun down beside his on the back of the four-wheeler.

Martin bent over and started picking up their spent casings. "Yeah. I don't know why, no one else does either, but you're a good kid, and once in a while, you're fun to hang around."

She stuck her tongue out at him from her squatted position on the ground before duckwalking away to grab a couple of stray casings.

"That's a good look on you," he said, and she rolled her eyes.

They worked in silence for a bit before she said, "I'm sorry. I was goofing off, and you were gonna say something."

"No. I was getting a little melancholy. Glad you redirected me."

"What were you saying about a voice? I mean, I have those too in my head sometimes. Most of the time, they're telling me to do something that I don't want to do."

"That's exactly what mine are saying."

"I figured. If it was talking you into coming home instead of staying out on the circuit."

"Yeah."

"So what are you hearing?" She stood, using her shirt as a holder, since there were too many casings for her to keep in her hand, and walked toward the four-wheeler. "Something like, you might as well quit because you're worthless?"

He stopped with a casing in his hand, staring at Bella, who lay with her eyes closed. "No. Not really. Nothing that bad. Just that, maybe what I've been striving for, and working toward, isn't what the Lord wants for me anymore. You know? And it makes sense to me. Like, at one time, being on the circuit was exactly what God wanted. I was sure of it. The last couple of years, it just hasn't felt right anymore. Even when I was still winning, at the beginning of last year, and the year before when I almost won the title. It still felt right. But by the end of last year, I felt like I should quit. Like God has a different plan for me now. It feels like I've done everything He wanted me to do there and like He's got something else. I just...just haven't been able to let it go."

She dumped her shirtful of casings in the box they'd brought and put her hands on her hips. "It's everything you've ever done. I get it. How do you forge a new life when everything that you've worked for in your life is pointed to what you're doing? How do you shift gears, change directions?" She gestured with her hand and shook her head, looking at the sky, trying to figure out exactly what she was saying. "How do you get a new goal and a new plan and something to fire your drive like what you've been doing all your life?"

"Exactly. It's like a funnel, and everything that I've poured in has been pointed at this goal—to win a championship. And now, it's like I need something new to point the funnel at."

"Exactly."

"You probably feel same way. You've hung your hopes on doing well in that audition and on being in the trick riding show for the next year and half."

"Yeah. That's exactly right. I guess it was a double whammy for me when I was driving home after my big screwup to hear that not only everything that I was working for had not panned out but had blown up in my face but that you were thinking about quitting too. I know I'm not you, but we've been so close through the years that your dream was mine. And to hear that isn't what you're doing anymore, it's been really hard to swallow. Along with my failure."

"Was it a failure?" He tilted his head, his cowboy hat shading his eyes.

"Feels like it. But I know you're going to be like my dad and say failure is just a stepping stone to success." The way she said it imitated her dad but was also half in a frustrated tone that said she didn't really believe it or didn't *want* to believe it. "But there *is* no other stepping stone. That was it. It's like not making the Olympics. You don't have a chance for another four years."

Martin nodded, and she knew he understood. "You might never have another chance."

"Thanks. That helps," she said with not a little sarcasm.

"You know what I meant." Martin didn't even look sheepish.

He didn't need to, because she knew he understood.

"Okay, enough on that depressing subject." She hunkered down and stroked Bella's forehead. "Our plans for the summer have kinda changed. I wanted to make sure we were still good with our agreement where I give you free slave labor for all the farm chores, and you allow me to continue to do my horseback riding and trick riding lessons on your property and stable my horses."

They'd had the agreement in place for years, but she didn't want to keep doing something that wasn't benefiting him anymore, so she tried to raise the issue a couple of times a year.

"You know that's fine. I've also talked a little bit to Pastor Race about having a few kids come over from the new rehabilitation ranch that Crew and Burgundy are starting. Some of the ladies there have children."

Blakely nodded, feeling Bella's warm, wet tongue as it licked across her palm. "Dad said something. He asked me if I'd be willing to give them free lessons. He even said the church might reimburse me some, but I told him it wasn't necessary. I hope that's okay?"

He squatted next to her, running a hand down Bella's back. "Whatever you do with your time and your lessons is fine with me. I'm just interested in your free labor for all of the work that we have to do around the farm."

"You know you can work me to death."

"And you love it."

"I do. I guess I probably do complain sometimes, but there's nothing in the world I'd rather do."

"I know. And you know, I've never had anyone else that I work with better than you. It's like you read my mind and know exactly what I want."

She put her hands to her forehead and hummed softly. After a couple of seconds, she looked up. "I'm feeling like you want lunch."

"See? I told you. Read my mind."

"We've got a list of stuff we can pick up in town. We could grab a bite at the diner. My mom texted me earlier and wanted to meet me there anyway. If that's okay." She pulled her phone out of her pocket and checked the time. "Your stomach growling is right on time. You have enough time to wash up and put Bella in the house. My mom said she'd be at the diner at eleven."

"Sounds like you might want to meet her first, and I can pick up the list of things we need at the hardware store and slip in after she's done talking to you."

She straightened and grinned at him. "Sounds like a plan."

Chapter Three

*B*ells jingled overhead as Martin stood in the middle of the feed store, grabbing a package of bolts and checking to make sure they were the nine-sixteenths that he needed.

He didn't bother looking up. He probably knew the person coming in. Mistletoe wasn't that big, but he was starving and didn't want to hang out at the store any longer than he had to.

Hopefully whatever Miss Penny had to say to Blakely wouldn't take long.

He should have grabbed a little something before they left his farm to tide him over, just in case.

His body still felt a little beat up from the rodeo, but that was nothing new. It seemed like when he was recovering, he was always hungrier. Must have something to do with whatever his body needed to repair it.

He wouldn't be having to worry about that anymore.

"Hey, Martin. Good to see you here. I was actually looking around for you. I'd hoped to run into you today."

Martin glanced up at the familiar voice. "Pastor Race. Blakely's supposed to be meeting your wife at the diner."

"They're there now. We have a new little girl with one of the ladies at the rehabilitation center, and I was picking a few things up for her, plus running a few errands. I thought I saw you walk in here, from the post office, and I was hoping I could catch you before you disappeared."

"I'm here. Doing my stuff so the ladies can chat. Although I'm hungry, so I hope they talk fast." Martin grinned, and Race laughed.

"I hope I'm wiser than to get between a man and his food. What I have to say won't take too long." Race's eyes crinkled, but he seemed to hesitate a little, as though he knew what he was going to say was going to be a bit of an imposition.

For some reason, Martin braced himself.

Race and Penny had done nothing but improve the town, and he, along with his whole family and everyone he knew, really, were appreciative of the work that they'd put into Mistletoe.

There was really no justification for the tightening of his back or the curl of premonition that made the hair on the back of his neck stand up.

"I mentioned our new charge, Darcy, and she has a brother, Frank. Krissy Evans has volunteered to take them to the rodeo which is the week after Mistletoe's Christmas in July festival. I was wondering...if you wouldn't mind going along. I know you're a big rodeo guy, and you can really show her the ropes. Krissy really doesn't know that much, so she'd appreciate your help."

Martin knew Krissy. Of course, he did. They had lived in the same town all their lives. But Krissy had always been interested in different things, running in different circles, and he'd never paid much attention to her.

Plus, she was a nurse. In his experience, she'd be telling him all the things he shouldn't do all the time, which was annoying.

Not that Krissy was annoying exactly, just nurses in general.

Martin spent enough time getting broken bones set and dislocated bones relocated into their proper positions, and he'd had a couple of hospital stints where he'd been there long enough to know that he didn't want to be there. And while the nurses were always kind, they were kinda bossy too. And they thought they knew better than he did what was good for him.

"I'll think about it and check my calendar."

He couldn't think of any other excuse not to do it. But he was pretty sure he could talk Blakely into going instead of him. Pastor Race seemed to be satisfied with his answer and nodded.

"The other thing I wanted to know," Pastor Race said as he pulled a notebook out of the back of his pants, along with a pencil. "I'm soliciting volunteers—last-minute emergency volunteers since the festival starts in a few days—to help with Mistletoe's Christmas in July festival. I was hoping I could put you down for something."

"Sure. Whatever you need help with. I'm there." He loved the festival and always helped, from the setting up to the tearing down. Each year, it had gotten bigger, and Mistletoe businesses had started depending on the tourist money it generated. Lots of western towns had festivals, but only Mistletoe had the authentic Christmas in July festival.

"That's fantastic. I'll put you down for the kissing contest."

Martin's stomach did three quick loops and then tried to jump out the back of his throat.

He opened his mouth, trying to figure out how to protest this without sounding panicked, because he could get on the back of a wild bronc with very little concern, but the idea of being in a kissing contest? And with who?

"I'll have you paired up with Krissy. She's the only one that doesn't have a partner yet. Thanks a lot."

The bell jingled, and Miss Penny stuck her head in. "Race? Are you ready?"

She remained in the doorway, accompanied by a solemn little girl with curly pigtails sticking out on both sides of her head. A little boy, slightly taller than the girl, stood behind them.

"That's my cue. I better get. Thanks for your help, Martin." Race grinned, and if Martin didn't know better, didn't know that he was a pastor and would never do such a thing, he would have said that his grin looked...gleeful.

He was really going to need Blakely to get him out of this. Somehow.

He bought the packages and hoped that he had enough presence of mind to get everything on the list, because his conversation with Race had upset him more than he'd like to admit.

Stowing the stuff in his pickup, he strode with purpose to the diner, more determined with every step to either come up with a way to get himself out of this kissing thing or go directly to Race and tell him that he was going to spend the next two months in Alaska and wouldn't be available to help with the Mistletoe Christmas in July festival, or the rodeo, or anything that had to do with nurses or kissing.

He loved the rodeo, but not with some woman he barely knew and who wasn't interested in the rodeo anyway beside him.

This was a mess. Whoever thought a kissing contest was a good idea anyway?

When he walked in the diner, "Silent Night," if he wasn't mistaken, was being played by a trio of horns over the loudspeaker.

He loved the constant Christmas music in Mistletoe. It just felt like home. Anywhere else he went, they played regular stuff, and of course that's what he listened to, but he knew it was Mistletoe if the thermometer read 85° and he was hearing "Silent Night."

Sometimes, it did become a little much, but not often.

Thankfully, Blakely was sitting in their regular booth, and he walked over and slid into the seat across from her.

"You don't look too much worse for the wear," he said as she glanced at him from staring out the window.

He supposed he spoke too soon though, because as she looked at him, her eyes were a little pinched, and her smile just wasn't quite as big as it usually was.

His eyes narrowed. "It wasn't good?" he asked, not waiting for her to respond.

She shrugged, her eyes looking down before her head swiveled back out toward the window.

"Don't keep me in suspenders, doc."

Mirth turned the corners of her lips up, but not for long. She played with the big bottle of ketchup on their table before she said, "They've got some kind of big-name football player coming to town." She sighed. Then her eyes lifted to him. "Have you noticed that my siblings seem to be pairing up and getting married awfully fast lately?"

That seemed to be an arbitrary question. But Blakely wasn't typically arbitrary, and he figured it must have something to do with everything that was going on. So, he thought back, tapping his finger on the table.

"Well, there was Ruby and that aborted wedding. Then she ended up with Ethan. Although Ethan isn't exactly your brother, everyone kind of assumes he is, like an honorary family member. And now being that he's married to Ruby, a real family member."

Blakely nodded and rolled her hand in the air. "Yeah, yeah, yeah. So Ethan got married, then Denver and Natalie somehow ended up together. Which I still haven't figured out, because Natalie was living in his house, but Denver is never home. How in the world could they get together when they weren't even around each other?"

"Good point. Denver really didn't spend much time at home. But then, there was West. He and Poppy, who I thought couldn't stand each other, all the sudden seemed to get together."

"Exactly. And then there was Crew, who isn't a family member exactly, but he's one of Denver's best friends, so he might as well have been. And he's gotten married." She lifted her brows and lowered her head, her voice lowering too. "See the pattern?"

Martin wasn't convinced, but Blakely was seldom dramatic, so he could go with it.

"I suppose. Is it a pattern?"

"I think so. And the reason I think so is because..." She looked out the window again. Her head nodded toward something in the distance. "See that?"

Chapter Four

Martin turned his head, trying to figure out what she was pointing at. And then he realized Race was standing on the sidewalk, gazing up at some dude who looked to be about twice as big as what a normal person should be, and they were chatting pretty intensely.

He made the logical deduction. "That's the football player?"

"It is. And my mom was just in here saying that she wanted me to go take the little girl—" She interrupted herself, which Blakely had a tendency to do, and nodded. "There's my mom. See the little girl?"

"Your dad mentioned her in the hardware store. Her name is... I can't remember."

"Darcy. Like Darcy in *Pride and Prejudice*."

"What? Pride in who? And Darcy? That's a town? In a story?"

"Never mind." Blakely rolled her eyes, looking almost like her old self. "The little girl's name is Darcy. And they want me to go with that big honking, oiled-up, slicked-up, completely worthless muscled football player to a horse show, taking the little girl because she likes horses, but—" Here, her head turned back to

Martin and her voice lowered again as she leaned toward him across the table. "What I don't understand is if they want me to take Darcy to a horse show, that's fine. I can do it. I'd like to. The little girl and her brother need help, love, and some good influences from what Mom was saying. But what I don't understand is why does the conceited, arrogant, full-of-himself football player have to go with me?"

"Whoa." Martin put both hands up. "Do you think we're getting a little hot under the collar here?"

Blakely blew out a breath and played with the napkin holder with the silverware, rolling and unrolling it in her napkin. She had the grace to look ashamed. "I know. I just...I just have such a hard time with people who only use their muscles to lift weights. I mean, I know there's a place for that, and it's not that I'm really looking down on them necessarily, it's just that it's not me. I want a purpose. If there is a purpose to your muscles, use them. But to just lift weights so that you can look big and toss a ball around, I'm not interested."

She had the silverware wrapped up so tight he could see the outline through the napkin. She sighed again, this one even more put out. "I couldn't tell that to my mom. Because she didn't exactly come out and say, 'hey, your dad and I are setting you up with this football dude.' She just asked me if I would go and take Darcy and mentioned that the football dude was going along."

"Maybe they feel like you need protection." Martin didn't really believe that, and Blakely's eye roll told him he probably should have kept his mouth shut. He couldn't think of any other reason why they would have the football player there, just as Blakely had said.

Blakely had rolled and unrolled her silverware again, and finally, like she couldn't wait for him to think any longer, she said, "I think they're trying to set me up."

Martin found himself fingering his own wrapped silverware. For some reason, the idea of Blakely's parents setting her up wasn't sitting well with him. He should be happy for his best friend. He always was happy when anything good happened to her. But... "I guess I don't really see this like a good thing."

"Me either!" Blakely exclaimed, like it was obvious.

"Good. Because I was feeling a little guilty for not feeling happy for you."

"I don't want you to feel happy for me!" Her silverware fell out of the napkin and landed with a clatter on the table.

She gathered it up immediately and began wrapping it again.

"I want you to help me figure out how to get out of this. I don't want to upset my parents. I know I can always tell them how I feel, and I know they have my best interests at heart, so I'm more concerned about hurting their feelings than I am about upsetting them and making them angry. Make sense?" She paused, and Martin noticed she gripped her napkin.

"I understand. I feel the same way about my parents. They always have my best intentions at heart. Sometimes though, they're really out there in the ideas they have."

"Exactly. And I'm pretty sure their idea is, somehow, that football player—"

Martin held a hand up, interrupting her. "Does 'that football player' have a name?"

"He does. But I might legitimize this process if I use it. So I can't."

"You're not making any sense, Blakely. Tell me his name. So we can use it, instead of calling him 'the football player.'"

"Fine. It's Dante. But to me, he's the oiled-up muscle guy that my parents..." She blew out a breath, her posture crumpling. "I'm sorry. I've not spoken kindly of him. It's nothing against him, it's just I don't want to be pushed on him. He's not my type at all. Surely they couldn't be thinking that we are somehow a good match."

"Gotta agree on that one." He didn't want to examine why, exactly, he didn't agree. He didn't really see anything wrong with the ballplayer, but he didn't want the man to be with Blakely. "I wonder if maybe your parents fell down and bumped their heads together or something?"

Her eyes lifted to his before dropping to watch as she shredded another piece off her napkin.

"What makes you say that?" she asked, rather abruptly, but he didn't take offense. Blakely was agitated. She also had a tendency to have a one-track mind when she had a problem in front of her. She'd work at it until she figured it out.

"Because your dad wants me to go with Krissy to the rodeo in three weeks."

"He what?" Blakely pointed the butter knife in her hand at him, like she was going to stab him.

"Take it easy with that stuff. I've spent enough time in the hospital. That'd be kinda hard on my ego, the bareback bronc rider in the hospital because his best friend stabbed him with a butter knife."

"Sorry." Deliberately, carefully, and very gently, she set her silverware down on the table.

He grinned, because almost immediately, she picked it back up and shredded another piece off her napkin.

"I think that stuff will make good fire starter."

Blakely's fingers didn't stop. "Just keep talking. They want you to go with Krissy to the rodeo?"

He nodded.

"That doesn't make any sense. Why wouldn't they have me go with you?"

"I guess it has something to do with the little girl. What'd you say her name was again?"

"Darcy," Blakely said absently as her gaze shot back out the window.

"Yeah. I'm never gonna remember that. I have no idea why they'd want me to do anything with Krissy. I'm not really into nurses. In fact, I'm definitely not into nurses."

"There's nothing wrong with nurses, Staples. Get over it." Blakely had sat through more than one of his rants on nurses being spawn of the devil.

"That's not what I said to you when you were going on about the oiled-up muscles of the football player."

"You're right. Okay, fine. I don't like football players. You don't like nurses. We can agree on that."

"Right. But that's not the worst of it."

More pieces came off her napkin. "That's not the worst of it? They want you to go to the rodeo with Krissy and Darcy, and that's not the worst of it? How could there be anything worse?"

"Oh, Whiplash." He shook his head, and her eyes widened.

He nodded.

"You know the Mistletoe Christmas in July festival's in a few days? Apparently, your dad is filling in the last-minute gaps of things that haven't been volunteered for. He had a chart and a pen and was taking names."

"I know. I got volunteered today while I was talking to Mom for a couple of contests. I don't even know what they are. I just agreed to it because I was so upset about the football player thing."

"Dante. You're upset about Dante."

"Whatever." Blakely waved her hand. Obviously, she really wasn't going to use his name. "What's the problem?" she asked impatiently, like she just couldn't wait to know what could be worse than what they had done to her with the football player and what they'd asked him to do with Krissy.

"Your dad signed me up for the kissing contest." He didn't have to pretend to be aghast. He still couldn't believe he'd gotten suckered into it.

Blakely laughed. But then she sobered quickly. "Like...not as a judge."

He shook his head.

"As a contestant?"

He nodded. "Yeah. I never thought about judging it. That would be an awful position." He paused, but then he added, "I suppose I would much rather be a judge than paired up with Krissy."

"You and Krissy?" Blakely said. "I can't think of two people less likely to ever be together."

"Maybe that's what your dad was thinking when he signed us up. Maybe he's trying to rig the contest so someone else wins."

"He would never do that." Her lips quirked. "Honestly, if you can get Krissy to kiss you, good on you."

Her words sounded like Blakely, the actual words, but the tone seemed a little strange. Which was odd. Blakely should be making fun of him up one side and down the other for this, but it seemed to upset her more. If that were possible.

"Krissy is a sweet girl and all, but I was really hoping you'd help me figure out how to get out of this. I don't want to be stuck kissing her. I mean, did she even graduate from high school yet?"

"She has to have. Dad wouldn't pair you with her if she hadn't."

"She looks like she's about twelve. I feel like I'm her dad or something. The idea is just gross." He put a hand up. "I really don't mean that as an insult to Krissy. I just...just would rather be set up with someone who's my age. Shouldn't she be kissing a kid that's still a teenager like her?" Martin's words were choppy and unsure. He really didn't want to insult Krissy. Even though he wanted to be very, *very* clear about not wanting to kiss her.

"I suppose we could try to start a petition around town and see if we can stop the kissing contest. That probably won't work though, because it's one of the most popular contests at the festival."

"I know. I've never actually even watched it though. I think it's mostly something that appeals to women."

Their waitress, Valerie, came over with her pad out, slightly out of breath. "I'm sorry it's taken me so long. Rush hour." She set down their normal drinks. "I knew you two are always talking a mile a minute about something and figured I could neglect you a little. Hope you don't mind, but I took the liberty of just going ahead and putting in your usuals. Did you want something different? It's not too late for me to change it."

"I was getting my usual. Thank you."

"Me too. My stomach is just about to walk itself back to the kitchen and start digging in the garbage can. So, anything you did to speed up the appearance of food on our table, I appreciate," Martin said.

"Seriously, Martin. Your stomach starts going through the garbage can, and I'm outta here." Blakely gave an exaggerated shudder.

"You'd better just keep that thing where it belongs if you want to eat today," Valerie said with a wink as she walked away.

"Valerie is more your age," Blakely said.

"She's as much older than me as Krissy is younger. I was hoping for someone I know…" He looked off around the diner. He really didn't want to kiss anyone. Not in front of the whole town plus a bunch of people he didn't even know. "They must be out of couples. Usually they have people who are married or engaged or at least like each other."

"Maybe they had trouble getting people to sign up this year? Or maybe they're expanding it?" Blakely suggested. And it seemed like she was striving for unconcern. It was really odd that she wasn't laughing at him. She'd help him get out of it; he knew her well enough to know she wasn't going to leave him hanging, but he expected her to tease him to death while she did it.

Funny that she wasn't.

"I guess I'll just have to man up and go talk to your dad and tell him I can't do it."

"I can't imagine they would rig it, but maybe they do have a winner they want, and they're pairing up other people who will definitely not work."

"Well, Krissy and I are definitely not going to work." Their eyes met across the table. "Boy, your parents really stirred things up today, didn't they?"

"I think that they've been in the business of stirring things up since they started the church however many years ago. They're not really afraid to step into anything, even stuff that other people wouldn't touch with a biosuit and a robot arm." Blakely stirred her finger through the shredded napkin in front of her. "And that's something I should be thankful for. If it weren't for their crazy willingness to jump into things that no one else will do, they wouldn't have adopted my siblings and me and kept us together and raised us as their own." Her eyes lifted to Martin's. "I'm gonna have to do what they ask me to do, just because of that. How could I not do what they want when they've done so much for me?"

Martin sat with his mouth closed tight, balancing his silverware on the ends between his two hands and studying the pieces like they held the answers to his life.

Finally, he said, "Being that you're my best friend, I wouldn't have you if they hadn't done that, which would mean most of my life experiences would have been completely different, so I suppose I need to do the same thing. They asked, and I need to do what they want. Just because they've done so much for my best friend, and I appreciate that more than I could ever tell or show them." He looked up, meeting her eyes and realizing that, maybe for the first time in his life, he wasn't telling her everything.

He didn't want to kiss Krissy. And true, she was too young, although not as young as he'd been insinuating—she'd gone to school with them and was just a couple grades back. But that wasn't the real reason.

Somehow, with the idea of a kissing contest—and, really, any contest—he always wanted to do it with Blakely.

Kissing was different, of course.

But as he looked at her, somehow his eyes seemed to drop to her lips, and he found that the idea of kissing his best friend wasn't as repulsive as it probably should be. In fact, there was some kind of shiver that went through him, giving him goosebumps up and down his arms and across his torso, and he thought that, maybe, kissing Blakely might actually be...nice.

Chapter Five

This trip to town certainly hadn't gone the way Blakely had planned. But sitting across from Martin, thinking about the kissing contest, was the worst thing about the entire day. Even worse than the idea of spending a day with that football player.

As Martin's eyes met hers, something seemed to change in them, and maybe because they'd been friends for so long, she felt like he was thinking about the same thing.

The idea of kissing Martin had never even entered her head before.

But then again, she'd never looked at his shoulders or seen the muscles rippling in his back and had any thoughts about them either.

But as his eyes darkened, and the expression on his face grew serious and almost...seductive, maybe, she found herself thinking that kissing Martin might not be such a bad idea.

She definitely could see it happening.

There had never been anything but easy friendship between them, but the air between them now seemed almost charged. It did to her, anyway. She wanted to pull her T-shirt away from her body and air it back and forth.

Why was she so hot?

And why did something that felt suspiciously like nervousness rip through her stomach and pull it tight like the drawstring on top of a bag?

Her mouth felt dry, and she licked her lips.

His eyes, which had been holding hers, lowered. Which made the tightening in her stomach almost painful.

So odd.

And then a thought, something so crazy, but something that felt so right, settled in her brain. And she had to pinch her mouth closed to keep the words from tumbling out.

She could partner with Martin in the kissing contest.

She shivered. A shiver so big she couldn't pretend it didn't happen.

"Are you cold?" Martin asked, his voice low and husky with a note in it she'd never heard before.

"No." Her own voice sounded weak and reedy and not like herself at all.

She needed to shake this. Needed to put some distance between herself and the kissing contest and thinking of her and Martin together in it.

"You and I have entered a lot of competitions together through the years," she said, striving—and failing miserably—for a casual tone.

"We sure have," he agreed, that husky note still in his voice. He seemed to shake himself a little, like he was pulling his mind back to their conversation. "When we pair up, we're pretty much unbeatable."

That was so true. They knew each other's strengths and weaknesses, and they worked together all the time. They knew each other as well as they knew themselves, almost.

"What if, what if we did what my parents wanted, kind of," she said slowly, her voice growing stronger as she ripped her eyes from him and gathered the torn pieces of her napkin into a pile. Studying that rather than meeting his eyes.

She didn't want to have any weird feelings for her best friend. If he didn't feel the same, it could ruin everything. And if Martin felt the same, he would have said something. He wasn't the kind of guy to sit around and not say exactly what he meant.

Then again, she wasn't that kind of girl either.

"What do you mean?"

She lifted a shoulder, the idea still forming in her head. Not feeling solid, but she didn't have to have solid ideas in order to talk to Martin. "What if we kind of trade off?"

He was quiet for a moment, maybe running her words through his head, but she waited without saying more, knowing that if she suggested it, he would get it. They always did get each other.

"Here's your food," Valerie said, and Blakely jerked back. She'd been so focused on Martin she had no clue the waitress was even coming.

"That's great. I'm starved," she said, almost breathless and trying to cover the fact that the waitress had scared her.

Martin smirked at her. He wasn't the slightest bit fooled. "My stomach was on its way to the kitchen. Good thing you intervened."

Valerie gave them a grin, her attention on him, like he probably knew it would be, giving Blakely a minute to get a hold of herself. The waitress set their plates in front of them. "You guys need anything else, holler."

They thanked her and prayed for their food, beginning to eat without saying anything more.

Finally, after Martin had finished three quarters of his hamburger, he said, "I think I get it."

Blakely laughed. "Be careful. You're reinforcing my hypothesis that men can't think when their stomachs are empty."

"That's not a hypothesis. That's proven fact. There's definitely science behind that one."

They shared an amused look.

Martin said, "You're thinking somehow you're going to go with me and the little girl—"

"Darcy," she supplied the name. Martin never could remember anyone's name.

"Darcy," he gave her a thankful look, "to the rodeo, and you're either gonna get Krissy to go with Dante to the horse show, or somehow, you're going to get me to take Dante's place."

Her smile had to be about ten stories high. "That's right. We can figure this out and work it to our advantage."

"Advantage?"

"At least make it so it's not to our disadvantage. Since you don't want to spend the day with Krissy, even though you like her and she's nice, and I don't want to spend the day with that football player...Dante..." she said his name reluctantly, because she really didn't dislike the man himself, "even though I'm sure he's a very nice person on the surface, although deep inside, I think there's probably nothing there but the vast amount of shallowness—"

"Stop. Someone might hear you talking and think you're serious."

"Sorry. You're right. He's a football player, so obviously he has deep intellectual abilities as well as wonderful physical prowess."

Martin rolled his eyes. "You're impossible."

"I'm sorry. I apologize to football players everywhere."

"And Dante in particular."

"Do I have to?"

"Do you want people to think that you're serious?"

"I apologize to Dante in particular."

"Heard my name."

A shadow fell over their table, and Blakely's heart dropped into her stomach.

"I thought I'd come over and introduce myself, but I guess I don't have to."

Blakely swallowed. Man, her smart mouth got her into trouble so often.

She risked a glance at Martin; he was smirking at her.

"I guess we don't have a lot of football players in Mistletoe. So you kind of stand out," she muttered, ashamed for her comments. Martin knew she was totally joking, but Dante wouldn't.

"Why? Do I have 'football player' tattooed on my forehead?"

Martin snorted, and Blakely shot him a look, one of her killing looks, which never had any effect on him, but she didn't know what else to do besides kick him under the table. She didn't want to hurt his bad knee.

"You're just shaped a little differently than regular people," Blakely said, with as much sugar as she could manage. Which probably wasn't much.

"You guys were talking about me. Good stuff, I hope."

There was a pregnant pause at the table. Blakely seldom wanted to lie. But this was one of those times. A lie seemed easier, but the truth was always better.

"I said something about manufactured muscles, and Martin insisted I apologize to football players everywhere and to you in particular. It makes me wonder if maybe he knew that you were there and didn't tell me."

Martin shook his head and held his hands up. "I wouldn't do that to you, Whiplash."

He would, but she believed him when he said he didn't.

"So you guys are having a conversation about football players? That's interesting," Dante said, with a touch of sarcasm in his words.

"Actually, we weren't." Martin gave Blakely a look that said he was coming to her rescue, and she owed him. Big time. "What we are actually talking about was that Blakely's parents had asked her to go to the horse show with you, and they had also asked me to go to the rodeo with Krissy. Which was unfortunate, since Blakely and I had been almost planning on going to those two things together, and now, with her parents asking us to separate, we were kind of disappointed that we weren't going to be able to spend those days together."

"Oh. You guys are a couple."

"No."

"Yes."

They stared at each other as their words came out together.

Blakely shook her head no, but Martin nodded.

Why had Martin said yes?

Regardless, he seemed to have this in hand better than she did, since she was already reeling from insulting the football player right in front of his face and mostly joking about it. But what she'd said hadn't been kind, and it served her right to get caught, she supposed.

Her hand, which had been fingering her fork, was suddenly covered by Martin's.

It wasn't that they'd never touched before. They'd worked together all the time, handing tools and bolts and wire back and forth between them. Halters, brushes, and whatever else they were doing on the farm. They'd touched plenty of times.

But never just for the sake of touching. Which was what this was.

His hand over hers, and hers sitting there, kind of like a scared rabbit, only maybe it felt more like a kitten. Wanting to turn and stretch and brush against his.

Absolutely ridiculous.

She was embarrassed at herself, but thankfully at least she didn't say that out loud.

"So there's some confusion about that?"

"No."

"Yes."

They really needed to get their act together. That time, she came out with the positive and he came out with the negative.

"So you look at me, think 'dumb jock,' and are deliberately trying to confuse me?"

"Yes."

"No."

She and Martin glared at each other.

"Maybe you guys could answer one at a time. I've got a feeling the second person's answer would change after the first person stated their opinion." He glanced between them, not seeming to take offense. "We do things a little differently in Michigan where I come from."

Martin cleared his throat. "I'm sorry." He held his hand out. "I'm Martin Zedler. And I truly am happy to meet you. I'm sorry things are a little bit weird. Blakely and I have had a really unpredictable day, and obviously, we're a little upset about it."

Blakely held her hand out, and Dante shook it without hesitation.

"I'm Blakely. And I really am sorry. Martin's right. We were being devious, and normally, we're a little crazy, but devious isn't really in our vocabulary."

"Blakely?" Dante said, with a tilted head. "Your dad is Pastor Race?" he asked, but it sounded like he already knew.

"Yes. Why?"

"Well, your dad had made what seemed like an odd request to me." Dante's biceps flexed as he ran a hand over his head.

"Oh?" Blakely said, trying to pay attention when she really wanted him to leave. Martin was basically holding her hand and she kind of wanted to...talk...about that? Or maybe just enjoy it. Which she couldn't do with Dante there, judging her for not loving football.

"Yeah..." His brows furrowed. "He said something about me being in the kissing contest with you."

Her fingers squeezed Martin's so tight, his were probably in danger of falling off. "I'm so sorry. I can't."

"Oh? Football players, huh?"

"I'm doing it with Martin."

To Martin's credit, he barely blinked.

Thankfully he didn't argue or refute her.

At least she didn't think he did. Blakely's brain was running laps inside her skull and she honestly wasn't sure exactly what else was said before Dante left what felt like hours later.

"We're in the kissing contest?" Martin said before the door had even closed tightly behind Dante.

"Yes?" her voice was a small squeak. "I'm sorry?"

His smile was real. And relieved.

"Better you than Krissy. I'll have to let your dad know. He was looking for a couple. I don't think he was set on who it was."

"I hope not...really? I'm better than Krissy?" Why was that the point that she had to come back to?

"Do I even need to answer that?" Martin asked. Then, without waiting for a reply. "Yes. Much. I'm comfortable with you. If I have to do something in front of the whole town, I'll pick you over Krissy every day of the week."

She wasn't sure what she was hoping for, but it wasn't exactly that. Still, "The same goes with me. Thank you for going along with that and not hanging me out to dry with Dante."

"I know how you feel about football players."

Chapter Six

Later that night, Blakely stood in Candy's stall, running the brush down her already shining coat, over and over again, mindlessly.

There was something so relaxing about stroking an animal.

And Candy didn't care how long Blakely brushed. She loved the attention.

Martin had something he'd needed to help his brothers with, and she was alone on his farm.

Which was what she needed.

Solitude.

Her happiness today hadn't been fake. Not really.

But it had covered the pain and disappointment and frustration at the Lord that she harbored in her heart.

Being a professional trick rider is what I worked for all my life. How could You have not given this to me?

On a regular day, even on a bad day, she was better than most of the ladies auditioning. That wasn't her being arrogant. Her stunts were harder and more dangerous.

Her horses were trained better than any other horses, and her work ethic was second to none.

She should have made the finals.

Her hand went down over the silky coat of her horse, following the brush. She tried to imagine why the Lord would have thought that she shouldn't have what she'd worked for her whole life. Why such a stupid mistake could cost her everything.

Why had He allowed that to happen?

Her phone buzzed, and she almost didn't answer it. She wanted to mope and feel bad for herself. But she pulled it out and recognized the number of Erin, who was a friend from the neighboring town of Spring Glen. She was also a fellow trick rider and a very good one.

She probably had made the finals.

Erin wasn't a great friend—they were competitors first—but Blakely still considered her a friend. She might need something, so Blakely swiped to answer.

"Hello?" she said, one hand holding the phone, one still brushing her horse.

"Blakely!" Erin's voice held excitement, then almost immediately, she toned it down. "I saw what happened. I'm so sorry for you."

Blakely had no reason to believe Erin was anything but completely sincere.

"I guess that just happens sometimes." She said it, and believed it, but didn't feel it.

"I know. It sounds like you're handling it okay."

"That's how I have to handle it." If Erin just called to rub it in, she hoped the conversation didn't last long.

"Well, I didn't want to make you feel bad, but I saw that you were definitely not going to make it, and then just five minutes ago, I got my call that I had made the finals! One week from yesterday, we'll be competing again to see who's actually chosen for the spot!" Her voice shook, and her words held bubbling exhilaration.

Blakely knew it made her a terrible person when her throat

closed up with what could only be jealousy. She and Erin had performed in parades and rodeos and festivals together, and Erin was good, but Blakely had always done the more technically challenging stunts.

"I was hoping, since you weren't going to be in the finals, that you would show me how you do the flipping out of your saddle trick? You know, the one where you do a flip after your horse stops and you land on your feet?"

It was the one trick she did that no one else could do. There definitely was a knack to it, a secret that she'd figured out years ago, ironically back before she'd even started competing, and it was one of the easiest ones she did. Once she'd figured out the secret.

She really didn't want to share.

Do unto others as you would have them do unto you.

She hated it when Bible verses popped into her head at the worst times.

Or best times, depending on one's attitude.

Her attitude hadn't been the greatest.

Who could blame her? She'd screwed up, lost the shot that she'd been hoping for and working toward, putting her heart and soul into, and it was gone.

Now you want me to help Erin, Lord? Isn't that pushing a little far?

You kept me from achieving the goal I've been working toward since forever, and now not only do I have to deal with that disappointment, but I actually have to help Erin succeed where I failed?

Aren't you expecting a little much out of me?

To whom much is given much is required.

She wanted to cross her arms over her chest and stand in the corner.

No, she wanted to curl up in a ball and cry in the corner.

"Blakely? Are you still there?" Erin's voice sounded tinny, since she'd dropped the phone from her ear.

She put it back up, knowing what she needed to say but not

wanting to. It was a matter of her heart being right but her actions not wanting to follow.

"Of course, I'll show you." She stopped way short of saying *I'd be happy to show you.* That would have been a lie too big to utter. "Anytime you want to come over to Martin's, you know I'm here from the time the sun comes up until after it goes down. Just show up."

"Don't you give riding lessons?"

"I'll work around them."

She'd canceled all her riding lessons for the week, because she thought she was going to make the finals, and she figured she'd be practicing.

Overconfidence on her part, she supposed.

Not really, because she should have made it.

"I'll be there tomorrow. Thank you so much." Erin's voice held all the eagerness and happiness of someone who was so close to seeing her long-held dream come true.

It held all the happiness and excitement that Blakely's would have held if she had made it.

She swiped off and threw her phone down on the bedding. The brush landed on top of it.

Candy nosed her, and she gave the elegant head a pat before she took two steps and dropped down on her knees in front of the wall, her forehead against the boards.

She didn't even know what to say to the Lord, and so she didn't say anything. She just let the tears that had been in the back of her throat since she'd screwed up and knew she wasn't going to be a finalist pour down her cheeks.

She'd never been a loud crier, so even though she knew Martin was gone and wouldn't be back until late tonight, her sobs were muted.

But she cried like her heart was broken.

Because it was.

She was angry at herself, for making such a stupid mistake, but she was upset with the Lord too, because He'd allowed it.

Plus, she was frustrated with the world in general. Not that she felt like the world owed her anything even though she'd lost her parents at a young age, because God had given her far more than she deserved, and she knew it. But she'd been working so hard.

Hard work was supposed to pay off.

You reap what you sow, Lord. Why am I not reaping?

Maybe you're going to reap something else.

Maybe this is Erin's turn to be victorious.

She didn't want it to be Erin's turn to win. She wanted it to be hers. She wanted what she'd been working toward. Not some other kind of stupid reward that she didn't even care about.

Don't you think I know how to give you what you need, and withhold what you want, if it's best for you? Don't you think I want the best for you?

Of course, He did. She knew it. It was just God's best always seemed to involve a lot of suffering. She was sick of suffering. Erin had two parents and lived in the house she was born in. Which is more than what Blakely had.

Why did Erin get even more?

Your parents are wise, and they share their wisdom with you. You have five siblings that love you. And a best friend that you can depend on no matter what. Knowing you have so much, are you really going to begrudge her this little bit that I've given her?

Immediately, the story of David and the sheep came to her mind. King David, who had everything, wanted more, and he took Bathsheba from Uzziah, killing Uzziah in the process.

I'm not killing anyone, Lord. It doesn't apply.

But she hadn't really been thinking about the lamb in the story the prophet Nathan had told David, because that really kind of did.

The rich man had herds and herds of sheep, thousands upon thousands, but needed a sheep for a sacrifice. Rather than using one of his own, he took the family pet of a poor man, the only sheep that man owned, using that as his sacrifice.

The principle was the same.

Someone who had everything wanting more, wanting to take the one thing from someone who had nothing.

She couldn't do it. She couldn't refuse to show Erin the trick and begrudge her the opportunity to win.

When Erin came, Blakely would show her everything she had. She'd give her everything she could, not just because God had given her so much, but because it was right.

It was right to encourage people.

It was right to share.

It was right to be kind, and it was right to treat other people the way she wanted to be treated.

Erin wouldn't do it for you. She's had plenty of opportunities to help you, and she never has. And she still won't, even if you do this thing for her.

That voice was familiar. It was her worst self coming out. The fleshly part of her that always was fighting for her own way.

It spoke truth. But she couldn't base what she did on what Erin had done or what she was going to do.

In her mind, it was easy to be sure she was doing the right thing, but her heart still hurt. And her tears still flowed, and her chest still felt like it ached with a pain that would never go away, because she would never have the opportunity to fulfill this dream again.

Her tears continued to flow, and her sobs continued to back up in her throat.

"Blakely?"

Chapter Seven

Blakely froze, her sobs stuck, before her hands desperately swiped at her cheeks, and she clambered, awkwardly because her legs were asleep, to her feet.

"Mom?"

What was her mom doing here?

It wasn't entirely unheard of for Penny to come and visit. Penny wasn't an accomplished horsewoman, but she loved Candy and Kisses, and when Blakely had a show or parade or competition, Penny almost always came out and helped groom the horses and even polish the chrome on her tack and season the leather.

Still, she didn't typically come out without telling her or just for fun.

Martin's barn wasn't exactly state of the art, and three light bulbs lit the entire stall area, which had irritated Blakely more than once before because it was hard to see anything at night, especially, but now she appreciated it.

Maybe her mother wouldn't notice that she was almost thirty and crying like a baby because she didn't get what she wanted.

It was embarrassing to think about. Definitely something she'd rather keep hidden, because it said so little about her character. Her *lack* of character.

"Hey, sweetheart. I figured I'd find you here," Penny said, coming to the door of the stall and stroking a hand down Candy's face while Blakely, having grabbed the brush, ran it down the silky neck.

"Always in the barn, I guess. Aren't I?" She still didn't sound quite normal. Her voice was a little husky from crying, and she was a little out of breath. Nervousness, embarrassment, and just scrambling to try to be her regular self.

"I suppose. This just seems to be your go-to spot any time you have a disappointment. And I know the competition was a disappointment, even though you probably feel like you can't show it."

She shrugged, trying to keep up the pretense it was no big deal.

She should have known her mom would see right through that.

"I know I saw you today in town, but I had Darcy, and I didn't want to talk about it in public anyway." Penny opened the door and walked through, closing it carefully behind her. With one hand on Candy's neck, lightly brushing down, she took another step forward and put an arm around Blakely.

Blakely hadn't gotten herself together enough that she could resist that light, gentle, compassionate touch.

Like the touch had turned the spigot back on, her tears welled up and overflowed.

She turned to her mom and wrapped her arms around her, burying her head in her neck.

"Mom, I wanted this so bad. I was so sure God was going to give it to me." Her words were muffled. She lifted her head and swiped at her eyes. "I practiced and worked and put everything I had into this. I was expecting big things from the Lord. And I was going to represent Him with my whole heart everywhere we went. Why?"

Her mom, wiser than she should be probably, didn't say anything but just pulled her back close and squeezed her tight, running a comforting hand over her back and stroking down her hair.

Long minutes went by as Penny allowed Blakely to cry as much as she needed to. Just holding her, soothing. Being that place where she could go when it felt like everything was wrong in the world.

Blakely didn't even need to tell her mom about Erin, about how God was asking her to give more, to be better than she thought she could be, when she didn't even feel like she could give up what He had expected her to give up with the competition.

Her sobs finally quieted, and her tears stopped flowing, but she hadn't lifted her head when Penny spoke.

"I know you know that every time, God gives us what we need."

Blakely spoke immediately. "I needed this, Mom. This was my whole dream."

"Sometimes, it's the personal victories, rather than the external victories, that we actually need."

Blakely didn't want to hear it, and she gritted her teeth.

"Sometimes, the growth that God knows we need can't happen if He gives us what we want."

"Don't you think I've grown enough? I lost my parents! He's given me enough trials."

Penny continued like Blakely hadn't spoken, not taking the bait to argue. "You can't control what trials you get. So many times, you can't control what happens in life, especially when it involves other people. That's in God's hands. What you *can* control is how you respond. You control how you love people. You control how you allow it to shape you. You control how you think. You control what you do, how you act. Don't fight the things you can't control. Fight for the things you can."

Blakely sighed.

Her mom knew her. She was a fighter. Struggling and striving, constantly trying to be better, constantly looking for new ways and things to improve. She lived and breathed and ate and slept horses and riding and even more for trick riding.

But that wasn't what life was made of.

And she knew it.

Her character, and how she developed it, was more important than any competition she'd ever be in.

It was more important than any show she'd ever auditioned for. How she acted was more important than winning.

She bit the inside of her cheek. "I know you're right, Mom. And I'm trying to make sure I act right. But my heart just isn't there yet."

Penny's head nodded against hers, and she leaned back until Blakely lifted her head and their eyes met. "Sometimes, it takes a little while for your heart to come around. No one expects a flesh wound or broken bone to heal in the day. Why do we expect a broken heart to heal immediately?"

"A broken heart makes it sound like I was in love."

"Maybe you were. Maybe you were in love with the idea of riding in that show or maybe just in love with the idea of acing the competition."

Blakely looked away. Either one was applicable. She was competitive.

"And that's fine. God wants us to do things with our whole heart. *Whatsoever thy hand find it to do, do it with thy might.* We can't bring glory to God if we do things and are lukewarm about them. God wants us to be on fire. He wants us to strive to be the best."

"That's only setting yourself up for heartbreak. Like mine right now."

"And that's what we're saying. Your heart hurts, but you're able to get yourself to do right. You can get your actions right and give your heart a little bit of time. If your actions are right, your heart's going to heal, and it's going to heal in the right direction. You're going to be better, because the next time this happens, it's going to be easier."

"I can't imagine this ever being easy. You can't put your whole heart and soul into something and be happy when things don't work out the way you want them to."

"You can learn to be happy that things are working out the way God wants them to. Especially if you respond the way God wants.

That's all he asks of us. He doesn't ask us to be the best in everything. He just asks us to love him with our whole heart. And to keep our eyes on Jesus."

Blakely backed away from her mom and leaned against Candy who brought her head around Blakely's shoulder and nuzzled her hair.

"I just can't see anything good coming out of this. But I can see all kinds of good things coming out of God giving me what I was working for."

"Whatever God has for you, it must be here in Mistletoe. You know, if you had secured a spot on that show, you'd have been gone from home for a year and a half. Possibly three years. Maybe that wasn't God's will for you."

Candy blew out her nose, stirring Blakely's hair, while Blakely thought about what her mom had said. She hadn't really even considered the amount of time that she'd have been gone. She'd just been determined to win a spot, because it was everything she ever dreamed of. She supposed how long she'd have to be gone would have been hard. Maybe she would have gotten tired of traveling all the time. Or maybe not. She could think of a lot of upsides apart from getting to perform every night—meeting new people and seeing new places and experiencing new things.

"Maybe my future husband is somewhere out there, and I'm going to be missing out on him, because I'm not."

Not that she was desperate to get married, but she wanted to eventually. She could think of all kinds of things that she could be missing.

Everything she'd thought of, all the positives, they were all gone.

"And maybe your future husband is right here. Somewhere in Mistletoe, just waiting for you to open your eyes."

She snorted. She couldn't help it. She didn't mean it disrespectfully to her mom, but that was ridiculous. Mistletoe was tiny.

"Trust me, Mom, if there was a man in Mistletoe that was

interesting to me, I would have snatched him up years ago." She met her mother's eyes. "And if you're talking about that football player, you can just forget about him. There is no way I'm having anything to do with someone that has more muscles than brains. Not interested. At all. And I'm sorry, you and Dad are pretty good at matchmaking, but not with me."

"Well, sometimes your dad does get a little overeager." Her mom's lips twitched a bit, like she was hiding a secret smile. "But I certainly would never match you with Dante. You're right about that."

"Plus, it's gonna take me a really long time to get over this failure." It was hard to imagine putting her whole heart into something again. Being interested in a man would take her whole heart, and it was pretty beat up right now.

Her mom put her hand up. "Don't think of it as a failure. It's been orchestrated by the Lord. He's got something in mind. Take it and turn it into success."

"How? There's no way I can turn not making that show roster into some kind of success! I'm back where I started from, only I've wasted a lot of time working on stuff I don't need and will never use."

"The girls you teach can use it."

"None of them are ever going to get to a competitive level. Very few of them anyway. Most of them are never going to use it."

"Don't close your eyes to the possibilities. Just keep them open. Look at the good."

Before Blakely could say anything, the barn door creaked, and confident strides that sounded like Martin's echoed back to the stall they were in.

"Blakely?" Martin's voice called out in the dark, dim lighting. "Miss Penny? Is that your car out there?"

"We're back here, Martin. In Candy's stall."

Miss Penny smiled at Blakely, a serene smile and maybe one that held a little hint of expectation in it. "Don't forget what we said," she whispered before she moved to the door and opened it. "I'm in here, Martin. You're right, I knew Blakely would probably be struggling, and I wanted to talk to her a little bit. I've barely seen her since she came back from the competition."

Martin shoved a hand in his pocket and adjusted his cowboy hat. "We did some shooting earlier today, Mrs. Steiner. I think Blakely needed to make a few pumpkins explode. Sure made me feel better, anyway."

"I'm sure it did, Martin," Miss Penny said, her tone wrapped with a heavy dose of humor. "It's late, and I'm leaving. Thank you for being such a good friend to Blakely." Her mom reached over and gave Martin a hug, which wasn't uncommon for her mom, since she was very affectionate. But Blakely, watching from the shadows of the stall over Candy's withers, felt like maybe her mom meant a little more by that than Blakely would expect.

What was she trying to say?

She shoved the thought aside. She couldn't fool her mom, but maybe she'd be able to fool Martin. It's possible he wouldn't know she'd been crying. Although, if there was one person in the world she could cry in front of, other than her parents, it would be Martin.

She trusted him with anything, even the depths of the disappointment she was feeling, that she couldn't show to anyone else.

Martin was a good friend. If nothing else, Erin deserved to win because Blakely had Martin, and Erin didn't.

Chapter Eight

Miss Penny walked out, and Martin didn't say anything. He hadn't needed more than half a second's glance at Blakely's face to know that she'd been crying. Which probably made him a terrible friend.

He'd taken her shooting, and they'd gone to the diner to eat, not that there was anything special about that, necessarily, but he'd wanted to make sure he took the time to spend just talking to her, in case she needed a shoulder.

He shouldn't have left her tonight.

Sometimes, he forgot that Blakely was a girl.

She'd never had a problem doing things with him, like the shooting and working beside him, outworking him on more than one occasion, but he supposed he'd really missed the mark on this one.

He should have told his brother he'd help him some other time.

Of course, he didn't know what he would have done. He hated it when Blakely cried.

It didn't happen too often, thankfully. But he should have been here for her. He should have known it wasn't just anger and frustration. Should have known there'd be hurt there too.

He knew how hard she'd worked, how big her dream had been, how much she wanted it.

He stood, with his hands in his pockets, just staring at the door, waiting. Not wanting to be the one to break the silence and start the conversation off. The conversation where he admitted he knew she'd been crying, and the one where, if she were being honest, she'd give him a hard time for not being the friend she needed today.

It hadn't been a terrible day. They'd settled some problems and had a few laughs, but he should have known her heart had been hurting.

Finally, he turned his head, taking a chance and looking at her. She had her head lying on Candy's back, one hand draped over her side, smoothing down the fur, and the other hand hooked around Candy's neck with her fingers buried in her mane.

At least her horse was there for her.

"Sorry I wasn't here," he finally said.

"You didn't have to be," she said, her voice muzzled a little because of her position leaning on the horse.

"You were crying."

"Maybe."

"I should have been here for you."

"I wouldn't have been crying if you were."

"I'm your best friend. Why would you hide that from me?"

"You know why. It's stupid. Just a big weakness. And there's no point anyway."

"Whoa. I know that tears don't help anything. But sometimes the hurt is just more than you can handle, and I should have known this was one of those times."

"It's not your job to know how I feel." Her voice didn't hold any anger or bitterness, and he felt she really meant it. "Plus, it was good for me to talk to Mom. She's right that we can't control the outcomes, but we can control our actions."

"Did something happen I don't know about?" He wasn't sure what she meant about her actions.

"I got a call—"

Like her words had conjured it up, her phone began to ring.

"What did you do, bury that in the bedding?" he asked, putting his head over the side of Candy's door, looking around for her phone, which sounded like it was coming from under Candy's feet.

"I dropped it, along with the brush, and never picked it up." She bent, swiping it from the floor and looking at the screen. "Oh my goodness."

"What?" He leaned over the top of the door, straining to see her screen.

She stared at it. "I think... I think this is the competition chair. I'm pretty sure that's their number. It's the right area code."

She lifted her eyes, and their gazes met.

"Answer it, Whiplash."

Hope had entered her eyes, and she fumbled the phone slightly while she swiped, then hit the button for speaker, ducking under Candy's neck and standing across from him on the other side of the door, holding the phone between them.

"Hello?" she said.

"Hello. May I speak to Blakely Barclay, please?"

"This is she."

"This is Laura Whitmire, of the judging committee for the traveling American trick riding association. I'm calling because you were just recently auditioning for our show."

"That's true." Blakely sounded like she wasn't sure what else to say.

Martin drew a face that made her laugh—a quiet laugh—and she lowered her brows as though warning him to quit it.

"Our tenth position finalist had to withdraw because she was in an accident on the way home. One of her horses had to be put down. She wasn't significantly hurt, and we offered to keep her spot open, but she withdrew because of losing her horse. After consulting with the rest of the committee, we decided to offer the spot to you. Your reputation was solid enough that we felt you had a bad break. Several of the judges know you, have seen you ride, and felt that you would be a great addition for our show. Basically, we'd like to ask you to come back next week and audition for one of the spots on the show."

Blakely's eyes had lit up, and she turned them, filled with wonder, on Martin. It caused him to suck in a breath.

He'd seen her happy plenty of times before, but there was just something about now. Maybe because of the other weird things he'd been feeling, but his heart kicked up a couple of notches, and he was tempted to touch her cheek instead of maybe throwing a friendly hand on her shoulder like he would have any time before.

His smile felt wooden, and he managed to keep his hands from moving, but Blakely didn't notice.

"I'll be there. Thank you so much for the opportunity!"

They didn't say much more before Blakely hung up.

"Can you believe it?" she asked, her red-rimmed eyes shining with enthusiasm and joy.

Martin nodded. "I certainly can. You're the best. They know it. I'm sure they want you in their show."

"I just... I'm overcome with gratitude." She paused, hesitating. "You won't believe this, but Erin Simpson called me and asked me if I would show her how to do my somersault after stopping trick."

She didn't need to explain the trick to him. He knew all her tricks, and that one was the best. It was the one that no one else could do.

"And you told her no, of course."

"That's just it. I didn't. I wanted to. I didn't want to help her at all, just jealousy and stupidity on my part, I guess. Being selfish. But I knew that I should. Because it was right. So I told her I would." She tilted her head. "Maybe this is God's way of rewarding me?" Her eyes sparkled, and she looked to him for confirmation.

He shook his head. "Maybe. I know God works that way sometimes. He might have just been testing you to see how you treat someone when you didn't think you were getting what you wanted."

"Exactly! And I passed the test, and He gave me what I wanted. I was sure of it before, and I'm even more sure of it now. I'm going to make the team, and I'll be touring the country in three weeks."

Somehow, the idea of all that didn't make him the slightest bit happy.

But he needed to be happy for Blakely's sake. So he would be.

Chapter Nine

The next day when Erin showed up, Blakely almost reneged on her promise. Now that she was back in the running, she wanted to keep her advantage to herself.

Erin certainly had never given her any hints as to how she did her tricks, and Blakely suspected if she asked, she'd have been turned down.

She didn't want to start a fight, and she didn't want to be petty or little. If she could help someone, she wanted to be the kind of person who would. She definitely didn't want to be the kind of person whose help was contingent on what they were going to get for themselves.

Still, as she walked Candy around the ring, and Erin pulled in, she was still struggling in her mind. Not really about what she was going to do—that was settled. But her heart was fighting her brain, trying to talk her out of the path she knew to be right.

If it's God's will for you to win, you're going to win whether or not you help Erin.

She knew that to be true. God could do anything.

Erin definitely had advantages. She was tall and slender and graceful. When she rode her horses, she just looked like she was flowing with them. Her long blonde hair, waist length and naturally silky, flowed out like a banner as she rode. That, along with her classic yet delicate bone structure, high cheekbones, and heart-shaped face... Erin was beauty and motion in the saddle.

Blakely looked more like a man pretending to be a woman and not doing a very good job of it, and that was on her best day.

She always figured she couldn't help how she looked, but she knew it mattered. Especially in the job she was auditioning for.

She hardly thought Erin could help her out with her looks. Erin had just been blessed with naturally good ones.

If Blakely helped her learn this trick, there wasn't anything Blakely could do that Erin couldn't do too.

Did she really want to give away her advantage?

Do unto others...

Yeah, yeah, yeah. She'd heard that a million times before, and she knew it. She shoved the verse out of her mind. Why couldn't she have a verse like *an eye for an eye and a tooth for a tooth* come into her head whenever she was trying to make a decision?

Well, that was one her flesh wanted her to be like.

In the smaller corral, Martin was working with one of the seven or eight horses he and Blakely were being paid to break and train. It was something they did on the side, around the ranch work, and it brought in enough money to pay for all of their feed expenses for their horses. But it did take time.

Almost as though he could feel her eyes on him, Martin looked up at Erin's car and then gave her a little thumbs-up.

Just to be smart, she gave him a thumbs-down, two of them, before she forgot her age and stuck her tongue out.

Right. That was just as mature as curling up in a ball and crying in her horse's stall last night.

Maybe when she hit thirty, she'd become magically mature, just because of the numbers beside her name.

She doubted it.

She could hope.

Martin rolled his eyes, then his attention went back to the horse he was working with.

Blakely led Candy to the side of the big corral and tied her up. She slid between the fence boards and walked over, greeting Erin and helping her get her horse, Peaches, off the trailer.

"I really appreciate you helping me. I truly was upset when I saw that you wouldn't be making the finals. You and I have done so many things together through the years. It would be nice if we could have done this together too."

Erin's words were all the right ones, but maybe it was Blakely's attitude, or the way her heart still hurt because of almost losing her dream, but there just didn't seem to be any warmth in Erin's eyes that would make her words ring true.

They felt like they were the right words but weren't backed up with the right feelings.

Blakely had done that herself more than once. She truly, truly meant the words. But just hadn't gotten herself to feel them yet.

She couldn't judge Erin for that.

"Actually..." She paused for a minute. Did she even want to tell Erin that she would be in the finals competition?

It wasn't like Erin wasn't going to find out. But it might change the dynamic of them working together today.

She decided to wait until before Erin left to say anything. She didn't want it to sound like she was bragging, and she also didn't want to make Erin feel uncomfortable.

"Yeah?" Erin asked, tightening the girth and not looking up.

"Nothing. Maybe before you go, we can chat for a bit, but let's get started now."

Erin nodded. "Thanks. I know you're probably pretty busy with lots of kids coming for lessons."

"I do have about twenty-five or so kids who come either weekly or biweekly."

She would have to give all those kids up, too, if she made the show. That thought had crossed her mind more than once, but there were plenty of places the kids could go for lessons.

Maybe there's something you can give them that nobody else can.

She couldn't believe she was that special. But she didn't argue with the voice in her head.

"I don't know how you get so many. If I get seven, I feel like I'm hitting a gold mine. I can't believe you have twenty more than that. Do you advertise?" Then Erin laughed, her hair shimmering as a breeze blew it softly away from her shoulders. "Never mind. I'm not looking to have to worry about that for a year and a half or more. I've heard they're really close to getting the European contract." Her lips smiled, and her eyes crinkled, but again, Blakely had an odd sense that she didn't mean it.

Maybe this was God keeping her humble. Maybe she was so sure she was better than Erin, because she did harder tricks, and she really wasn't. Or maybe she was just used to excelling, and she needed to remember how to be happy and humble when other people were doing well.

Or maybe it's something else. Something basic that you're forgetting.

The thought stopped her cold. What basic thing could she be forgetting?

Reminding herself to be very careful to be nice, that it wasn't Erin's fault she made a huge mistake, she did her best to give a sweet smile. "You have a lot to look forward to. I don't know how far your kids drive, but if you want to recommend me to them, I can handle five or seven more kids."

"I'll do that," Erin said, somehow making it sound like she was throwing a couple pennies in Blakely's direction.

God resisteth the proud but giveth grace unto the humble.

Blakely figured she could use all the grace she could get. She could also definitely use these lessons in humbleness.

Erin walked beside her, leading Peaches, as they went to the gate and Blakely opened it.

Erin flipped her hair over her shoulder. "Of course, I would trade all of my kids for the opportunity to work with Martin. Maybe you can put in a good word for me."

"You could be gone for a year and a half." Irritation made Blakely's words shorter than she intended.

"Maybe absence makes the heart grow fonder? Plus, there's Skype, FaceTime, and Zoom. Plenty of ways for us to see each other. If he's really interested, he'll come see me. I think he'd enjoy it. Sometimes, we have a tendency to let ourselves be stuck on the farm all the time. And now that he's not chasing the rodeo, he should have time for a girl." Erin's eyes lingered on Martin as he moved with a fluid grace, speaking in a low tone, working with the horse.

"I don't know if he'll be able to stay away. It's in his blood."

"Maybe he'll get a girl in his blood." Erin winked before walking through the gate, and Blakely closed it behind her.

She supposed she could let Martin know that Erin was interested. He didn't have a clue, she was sure. And who knew, maybe he really was going to be looking to settle down now that he wasn't on the circuit anymore.

Somehow, having Erin get both the position she'd dreamed of all her life *and* her best friend didn't really sit well. And she couldn't quite bring herself to trust that this second shot at the competition would go any better than the first. As bitter as she felt toward the Lord, she wouldn't be the slightest bit surprised if He made her give it all up. Her position, her best friend...

Lord, do you want me to give her my horses too?

She was being sarcastic and not respectful, and she regretted it immediately. God didn't deserve her sarcasm. He definitely didn't deserve her bitterness either. Still, she could hardly combat the desire to stand with her arms held up to the sky and just say, "Hit me again, Lord. Go ahead. Hit me again. Harder. Give me the best shot you've got."

Yeah, talk about asking lightning to strike one dead.

Still, that's how she felt. Like He was just going to hit her again and again, just as hard as He could, until He finally knocked her down.

Where the compassion of her mother and the concern of her friend hadn't helped, just the idea that she needed to fight to stay on her feet squared her shoulders and straightened her backbone.

She might get knocked down. But she would be back up fighting, and it wouldn't take long. And she'd keep fighting as long as it took. There was *nothing* that could knock her down and keep her down.

And she would be nice while she was doing it.

Fixing Candy's reins, then putting her foot into the stirrup, she swung up into the saddle.

She opened her mouth and forced the words out. "Now, I'm going to tell you something I've never told anyone but Martin: the secret to the stop and somersault trick."

Erin's eyes lit up. Yeah, this was the whole reason she was here. "I won't tell a soul."

Blakely didn't trust her. She figured someday she'd be selling the secret, because, once she did it long enough, it would feel like her own. And she'd forget.

Still, Blakely wasn't going to hoard what God had given her. Her heart was broken, it hurt, her chest felt like it was filled with rubble and she honestly wasn't sure where in the world she was going from here. Plus, she felt bitter toward the Lord for allowing all the pain she was feeling, but she wasn't going to let her bad feelings stop her from doing what she knew was right. Even if it was hard.

She forced the words out. "The secret is: you gotta stay loose. Almost relaxed, maybe even doll-like. Think of yourself as a rag doll. Now, of course, you move with the horse when they're cantering, and your body feels fluid that way. But we have a tendency, when we know we're going to go into a big stop, to tense up. Right?"

Erin nodded, her face set in lines of concentration, hanging on Blakely's every word. In just a few seconds, comprehension dawned over her face. "You let the momentum from the horse throw you into the somersault."

"That's exactly right. You've got to stay loose, the horse begins to stop, you tuck your chin, hunch your shoulders just a little, not enough to break form, and then the momentum from the horse does everything else. And you end up planting both feet right by her front feet, and your heads are aligned."

"Sweet." She said it with such satisfaction the word was two syllables. "I knew there was a key, something I was missing. You wouldn't believe how many times I've tried this at home, and every single time, I've landed on my butt or my head."

No, Blakely *could* believe it. She'd spent plenty of time trying to learn other people's tricks, and the same thing had happened to her—she spent most of her time picking herself up from the ground.

But she'd mastered each and every trick she'd set out to learn.

For the next two hours, they alternated working on the somersault trick, which, now that Erin knew the secret, only took her six tries until she landed on her feet. They also practiced some other tricks that Erin felt Blakely did better.

Martin eventually put his horse away, and for fifteen minutes he'd been standing at the fence, one foot on the bottom rail, with his forearms hanging across the top. Watching.

Erin definitely went into performance mode when she noticed Martin at the rail.

Blakely was tempted to laugh, but then she took a good look at Martin, seeing him, maybe through Erin's eyes.

With his cowboy hat pulled down low over his head, his broad shoulders filling out his shirt, and the manly pose that screamed casual strength, she could almost feel her own heart somersaulting in her chest.

But it was Martin. She had to remind herself a couple of times before the butterflies in her stomach stopped trying to escape.

That's just what she needed to make everything worse. She'd lose her best friend, but not because of Erin, because of herself and her stupid, weird reaction brought on after realizing someone else found him attractive.

She was kind of disgusted with herself for that. Why did someone else seeing him as attractive make her realize that, yeah, her best friend was a good-looking man?

"I can't take up any more of your time. I appreciate all your help." Erin pulled her hair back out of the ponytail she'd put it up in when they started before slapping her hat back down on her head. "I'm gonna try that trick one more time." She raised her voice and called over to the fence, "Hey, Martin, watch this!"

She urged Peaches into a canter. Her blonde hair streamed out behind her, and her pink cheeks and long, graceful lines made her seem like one with the horse and the wind. She executed the trick perfectly, sliding Peaches to a stop, tucking her chin, hunching her shoulders, somersaulting out of the saddle, landing on her feet, and lifting her hat off with a flourish all in one smooth motion.

It was a true sight to see. Erin definitely had more natural talent in her little finger than Blakely had in her entire body.

Her technique might not be as good as Blakely's, and Blakely might be more aggressive and more willing to take risks and ride the edge, but she could never get herself to look that beautiful, no matter what she did. It was just something Erin was born with.

Martin slow clapped at the woman standing right in front of him. "Nice job. You do it almost as well as Blakely."

Blakely's heart stopped.

Erin beamed. "Thank you. Maybe you can find some time between your chores to come on over to Best Bet Ranch, where I board and train, and you can give me a hand with my last-minute prep. I know you know how, because you've helped Blakely win her trick riding competitions."

Blakely looked at the ground between Candy's ears. Martin had been on the circuit more than once when she'd been getting ready for a competition, and she knew how to do it by herself. She also knew that she could get Journee to come out and help her, although her sister wasn't nearly as fond of horses as she was.

She had plenty of resources, and Erin probably didn't.

Blakely didn't need Martin.

She just wanted him. Because he was supposed to be her friend.

Maybe Martin was looking at her; she didn't raise her eyes to see. She wanted to turn and leave, but she didn't want to allow the shallow part of herself to win.

Only a couple of seconds had elapsed since Erin had finished talking before he said, "Blakely didn't tell you about her news, did she?"

"What about her?" Erin asked, her brows drawn down.

Martin didn't say anything, and Blakely raised her eyes. There were questions in his. She looked at his shoulder, then turned her eyes to Erin.

"I didn't want to tell you when you first came because it might have made things weird." Blakely stroked Candy's neck, soothing herself more than the horse. Erin didn't look happy.

"Tell me what?"

"Blakely is going to be in the finals competition too." There was pride in Martin's voice. It made her stomach feel like she swallowed a helium balloon. "They called her last night saying they had an opening, and they asked her to step in. Which, of course, she did, because this means everything to her." Martin's smile was sincere, and it did reach his eyes, and she didn't question, not for one second, that he was happy for her.

Their gazes met, and something seemed to shift between them. She couldn't put her finger on it, but along with their long-standing friendship, something else flowed between them. Something sweet and new, it seemed to shimmer around, warm and soft, making her feel light and happy. It was all she could do to keep herself from starting toward him.

"Are you sure you won't have time to help me?" Erin asked, her voice sounding like warm honey. "Of course, I understand if Blakely is your priority. I can find someone."

Martin didn't say anything, and Blakely almost opened her mouth. She wanted to tell him that he could just go ahead and help

Erin, it was her natural inclination, but that wasn't what she wanted, and Martin was old enough to make his own decision.

She kept her mouth closed.

"I'm sorry, but you're gonna need to find someone else. There's no way I'm helping anyone but Blakely." He lifted his hat and ran a hand over his hair, something he did when agitated. "She's helped me for years, for little or no pay. I've been strapped more than once during that time, and honestly, I wouldn't have a ranch without her. Just wouldn't. I owe her everything."

Blakely had to step in. Her focus was Martin. Honestly, she pretty much forgot Erin was even there. "You don't have to help me just because you think you owe me. You know I've enjoyed every second of the work we've done on the ranch. And while it might be true that you wouldn't have it without me, it's also true that you allow me to make a living on it by giving riding lessons and letting me board my horses for free." Not to mention neither one of them could break and train the horses that they did alone. So many things took two people. "I think we work well together."

She didn't know why she added that last bit, but it came out softer and felt like her heart was speaking.

Martin's eyes darkened, and they lingered on hers. It felt like he was speaking without saying anything.

Erin cleared her throat, breaking whatever conversation Blakely and Martin were having without saying anything.

Martin looked at her. "Okay. Let me rephrase, because I don't want to be unclear. Blakely is my best friend; my loyalty is with her."

Erin swallowed, and Blakely felt bad. Martin's words, while they helped her sore heart, had to have been hard for Erin.

"Maybe I'll be able to come over and give you a hand," Blakely said.

"That'd be rich. We're competitors. How would I know for sure that you're actually helping?" Erin's words sounded bitter, and her face twisted, marring her perfect beauty.

"Do you think what I did with you this afternoon was something that I'm doing to sabotage your chances?" She'd just given Erin a secret that she'd never shared with anyone, and Erin was acting like she was the enemy.

Erin's eyes dropped. She seemed to deflate on her saddle, although she still looked regal and beautiful. "I guess not. It's just, I know it's not uncommon for people in small towns and in the rodeo circuit to help each other, all the time. But it is a little unheard of for people to make the sacrifice you've made. You have to admit no one is this generous or giving. Especially without me offering you anything in return."

Blakely really didn't want to get into her struggle. Not with Erin. She could talk to Martin about it. Or her mom. Even her dad, and a few other friends, maybe. She didn't want to be that vulnerable for Erin. She'd already been humble.

"I don't think I did anything that anyone else wouldn't have done." She was ready to end this conversation. It was exposing too many feelings she wasn't sure she could deal with. "Come on, we'll untack and I'll help you load Peaches."

It was another hour before Erin pulled out, and Martin had wandered off.

Blakely guessed he was probably hooking up the tractor and making sure the blades were sharp on the mower, since he'd mentioned cutting hay the next day. Sure enough, she found him in the small, dark equipment shed, sharpening the blades.

She walked to the door opening and stood there.

"You're in my light."

"There's no light in there."

"Sounded good."

"Thanks for what you said back there. I appreciated it." It was the sole reason she had sought him out just now. Normally, she would have started feeding the horses, mucking out stalls. But she needed to let Martin know that she wasn't taking what he said for granted.

"It was the truth. I meant it." His hands pulled back from the grinding wheel, and he flipped the switch, turning it off, the blade held in one hand. "I know Erin isn't your favorite person right now." He held a hand up when she opened her mouth. "And I know that you'll eventually get over that. I know you're going to do the right thing, I know you're gonna *feel* the right thing. And I appreciate your transparency in not pretending that this is easy for you or that you're some kind of super spiritual giant that does everything right the first time. I just know you make me proud. Because there's something very gratifying in being associated with someone who puts other people first. Even when it's hard."

"I was talking about you saying about your loyalty."

"That's where it is. It's with you. We've been friends way too long for me to put you aside for someone else. Plus, I think we work well together." He grinned at her.

She'd cried more in the last two days than she'd cried in her whole life before. There it was in her throat again, clogging it with a big lump.

"Thank you," she said, her words coming out in a whisper. "That's all I can say. Thank you."

"You don't need to thank me. Because I know you'd do the same thing for me. Even more, I know you'd fight for me. You're a fighter. Plus, I really do owe you after everything you've done for me. What I said to Erin was true. I wouldn't have this ranch without you. Honestly, if I were being right and fair, your name would be on that deed as well. Because you put just as much blood, sweat, and tears into it as I have."

Blakely pulled both of her lips in and pressed them between her teeth. She looked at the blade Martin held. "I didn't do any of that for any special privileges. I didn't do it because I wanted my name on any deed. And I didn't even do it because I wanted any kind of special accolades or anything. It's just always been fun. And I want to see you succeed."

"Then why is it so hard for you to believe the same of me? Because I can say that exact same thing. It's always been fun, and I want to see you succeed. And I'll choose you over Erin and anyone else in the world, any day of the week."

Her eyes shifted to his, and their gazes met over the distance that separated them. Despite the darkness, despite the tears welling in hers, despite the hurt and the hardness of what she'd done, that same thing from before seemed to shimmer and shift in the air between them. That thing she'd been noticing the last few times she'd been around Martin. It had something to do with the attraction she felt and the new light she was seeing him in. It was dangerous to their friendship, and she tore her eyes away.

"I guess I'll get started on the feeding. I just wanted to thank you."

"The feeling's mutual," Martin said.

She nodded without meeting his gaze again and turned, walking away from the equipment shed and the man who was starting to feel like more than a best friend.

Chapter Ten

Sweat trickled down Martin's temple as he settled the portable corral panel in place. Blakely was at the other end, of course.

Her dad asked her to do a little exhibition for the Christmas festival, and Blakely took the chance to use it as practice for her audition the next week.

Of course, Martin had volunteered to help her set the corral panels up.

He needed to keep busy so he wasn't tempted to think about the rodeo he was missing. Although, if he were being honest, he didn't miss it nearly as much as he thought he would.

He'd enjoyed working with Blakely. He'd been something close to disappointed when she'd gotten that phone call saying she was back in the running for the position in the show. He wasn't sure he'd be happy at his ranch if Blakely wasn't there.

He'd started thinking about having her there all the time. Which meant he was thinking things he shouldn't. But he might as well admit it: his admiration for Blakely was turning into something deeper and stronger than just friendship.

It was true she did go after what she wanted and was never shy. But it was also true that she constantly put other people ahead of herself, and a lot of times, people took advantage of that.

Erin definitely had this week.

It was unheard of to ask someone to show them their secret trick.

It was even more unheard of for someone to actually do it.

In his opinion, Erin didn't really deserve the kindness that Blakely had shown her, but it wasn't up to him to judge.

And he certainly wouldn't judge Blakely, because she was right. It was right to treat other people the way he wanted to be treated, no matter who those people were and no matter what they did to him.

An easy lesson to learn, but it definitely wasn't an easy lesson to live out.

Blakely did it all the time.

She was competitive, and she rode with her heart on her sleeve, hard and fast and risky, but she was kind and sweet and nice too.

And despite her tough exterior, he'd seen her soft underside enough to know people hurt her more easily than what they thought.

She put on that tough persona, and everyone assumed that's what she was.

Probably because she wanted them to.

"One more panel will do it," Blakely said as she walked up to him, closing the distance between them, waiting for him to straighten and look at the almost completed corral before they went to the trailer together to grab the last panel.

It was definitely a two-person job.

"You sure you don't want to farm this out a little longer? Seems like your dad's been hanging around with Dante, ready to pounce as soon as you're available."

He found that mostly funny, but it also bothered him some on a level he didn't want to examine.

What did he care who Race and Penny wanted to pair their daughter up with?

Except, she was his best friend, and he knew for a fact she wasn't interested in any football player.

Although, he supposed it bothered him a little bit, because he couldn't think of any kind of man she'd be interested in.

Other than him.

And of course, he certainly wasn't going to break the laws of nature and fall in love with his best friend. He didn't want to ruin the great friendship that he and Blakely had, so—laws or no laws—Blakely was off-limits for him.

But she was also off-limits for Dante.

She didn't want him, and Martin would help her make sure she didn't have to have him.

"Very funny." She lifted her hat and shoved her hand up over her forehead and back across her hair, flattening the strands that wanted to fly away before shoving her hat back on her head. "After we're done here, we can discuss strategy on the kissing contest. We don't want to do it so well that we win."

Martin nodded and coughed at the same time. "Definitely not."

The winners were teased for weeks afterwards; anytime they showed up together, people would ask for an example of the winning kiss.

"One kiss is going to be awkward enough," he added. "We definitely want to put some strategies in place to make sure that we're not too good at it."

"Exactly." They lifted the panel, flipping it down and turning it a little so she was walking forward, but she talked over her shoulder. "I figure that we need to look awkward and embarrassed, and we definitely need to fumble around a lot."

"I guess."

"What do you mean 'you guess'?"

"I gotta be honest, I've never actually watched the kissing contest. I have no idea what kind of kisses the judges want."

"We need to think like the judges?" She threw a look over her shoulder that said she didn't believe it, but she was thinking about it.

"I don't know. I really don't. And up until last week, I didn't care. I mean, come on. Who actually watches the kissing contest?"

"Dad said it was the most popular contest in the festival."

"That means everybody's grandma and their great-aunts are there. Surely men don't actually watch that."

"It's probably like romantic movies, right? The ladies drag their men to them, and they're forced to watch."

"I don't think that most men have a problem actually being in the kissing contest, it's just watching it that's gross."

Blakely stopped so abruptly that he pushed the panel past her arm and into the ground before he realized it.

"Sorry. What's the problem?" He searched for what might have made her stop, seeing nothing on the ground in front of her that could cause any problems.

"You said some things that were so crazy that I just had to question your sanity."

"We can argue about this, but I think you're just as insane as I am."

"People do say we're two peas in a pod."

"Exactly. So if I'm insane, it doesn't bode well for you."

"But I don't have a problem watching kissing contests. And what is this bologna about men wanting to be in the kissing contest?"

"Well, that second question is pretty easy. Men like doing the kissing, not watching it."

Blakely glared at him out from underneath the rim of her hat. "I think this is a subject we've never spoken about before." There was a little bit of wonder in her voice, like she could hardly believe it.

He supposed he shared that wonder, in a way. He and Blakely talked about everything. Seriously. Everything.

But not kissing.

"Well," he said slowly, because he just realized he'd made a blanket statement, and it might not be true. "I guess I can't speak for every man on the planet. And kind of like you and I have never actually talked about the kissing word, I don't go around talking to my buddies about it either. Maybe I'm wrong. Maybe men really don't like kissing. Maybe being in a kissing contest isn't something that they'd volunteer for."

"You didn't want to do it when it was you and Krissy."

He couldn't deny it. He hadn't even seen that big, gaping hole in his logic until she just now pointed it out.

She didn't press her advantage, and her look remained thoughtful. "I suppose kissing is probably okay, but doing it in front of a bunch of people doesn't sound like a good time to me."

"I think maybe if you're kissing the right person, the audience doesn't matter."

"I wouldn't know," she said, kicking the dirt, then picking the panel back up.

He had to scramble so she wasn't dragging his end on the ground, but he also had to smile a little. Blakely was so consumed with horses and riding that she'd never really thought about boys too much.

Maybe that was why her parents felt like they had to pair her off and bring Dante in for her.

At the very least, being in the kissing contest had stirred her up.

His smile dimmed. He didn't really want their relationship to change. He liked that Blakely wasn't interested in guys and had never gotten boy crazy like other girls in school.

She'd made it almost the entire way through her twenties without being afflicted.

He supposed it was selfish of him to hope she never did have that issue. She'd probably want a husband and children just like about every other person in the world eventually.

Some lucky guy would get a pretty great girl. And, as these things went, he'd lose his best friend.

"Maybe I can do some scouting around. Maybe we can figure out what kind of kiss won last year and what kind of kiss came in last place. That could help us with our strategy. And I know just the person to ask."

"Journee."

She laughed. "That's right. If anybody's a sincere romantic and has never missed a kissing contest in her life, it would be Journee. She'll give me the lowdown. Although I'll probably have to act like I want to win the contest, which won't be too hard for her to believe, because for some reason, everybody thinks I'm competitive."

She shrugged her shoulders and rolled her eyes a little while he outright laughed.

"Blakely, that's because you are."

Chapter Eleven

Blakely barely turned away from Martin and picked up her end of the panel again when her eye caught on the ladies setting up the pie tables.

Not necessarily on the ladies, but she saw her mom with two silent little children beside her. Her mom looked slightly frazzled as she gave instructions to the ladies. The plastic tablecloth two tables down was being whipped by the wind. It billowed up and almost blew away.

Her mom, grabbing for the tablecloth, bumped into the silent curly-haired girl at her side. She reached her hand down and wrapped it around her shoulder, keeping her from falling, while slapping the cloth back down on the table with the other hand.

"Hey, Martin?" Blakely said as her friend settled the last panel in place.

He stopped and straightened. "Yeah?"

"Didn't you say you were going to help set up the temporary pens and sort animals?"

"Yeah. I promised Sam and Dallas that I would."

"Rather than trying to find Journee, I'm going to go see if I can give Mom a hand. If not help, at least take the kids and walk around with them a little." The fair didn't start until the next day, but there were plenty of things to see.

As she thought, Martin nodded, his eyes shifting over to the ladies at the pie tables. "That's the best thing to do. If I get done, I'll come look for you. If you want to bring the kids over and think they'll enjoy watching the animals, we'll find a good spot for them."

"Okay. I probably will. I always loved to watch that when I was a kid."

"You were always in the way, too."

She put her hand on her hip. "I was a bigger help than you were. You were scared of all the animals except for the rabbits."

"That's not the slightest bit true. Although I do know you can't herd rabbits."

"It's as hard as chickens, that's for sure. Make sure those cages stay tight shut."

They gave each other knowing grins, both of them probably remembering the time that some teenage boys, everyone assumed on a lark, had opened every single rabbit and chicken cage in the festival. It had taken a ton of volunteers an entire afternoon to try to get the animals caught and sorted and back where they belonged.

They weren't entirely sure that everyone had ended up with the chickens that they'd started with, since chickens, especially, were hard to tell apart, but they did their best. And they definitely both learned that day that chickens nor rabbits herded like cows and horses.

Of course, it didn't hurt quite so bad when a chicken or rabbit stepped on one's toes either.

Martin put up a hand, and Blakely returned the gesture before turning and starting toward her mother.

When she reached the table, her mother had just gotten the tablecloth straightened back down and held it with one hand on either end of the table, slightly bent over while someone else was taping underneath.

"I was wondering if I could walk around with the kids for a little bit?" Blakely asked.

Her parents had never stopped being foster parents, and it wasn't unusual for them to have an odd assortment of children running around now that most of the Barclay kids were out of the house.

They'd talked about adopting more, but it just hadn't worked out.

Still, Blakely was used to giving her parents a hand with the kids they were fostering.

Her mom lifted her head, a look of relief mixed with humor on her face as she continued to bend over the table, spread eagle, holding the cloth down. "I think they would much rather hang out with you for a little bit than stand here with me. I didn't realize I was going to be doing this now."

"I'm more fun than my mom." Blakely wrinkled her nose at the two serious children. The little girl didn't crack a smile, but the boy sure did.

"Wherever Dante is, I'm sure he would help you." Her mom kind of looked around, and Blakely spoke quickly.

"I'm fine. I think these kids can handle me."

"I want to talk to him! I've never met him before! I've seen him play on TV. He's super cool. I want to be just like him when I grow up." The little boy practically jumped up and down.

Still, seeing someone famous had a tendency to do that even to adults.

"Maybe Blakely will take you and introduce you to him. I think your dad was saying that you two might go to a horse show together. Dante's never been, and there's no one better to introduce him to everything than you."

Blakely pressed her lips together and nodded, trying to look happy and not guilty. She was a terrible actress.

"You can go ahead and stand up now, Miss Penny. I've got the tablecloth taped down tight," Mrs. Walter said, standing up slowly with a hand on her back.

Maybe she should have offered to help with the tablecloths. She dismissed the idea. The kids needed her more.

"This is Darcy, and this is Frank," Miss Penny said, putting a hand on the girl's head and one on the boy's head. "This is Blakely, and she's one of my daughters. She does know Dante, so maybe she'll introduce you to him, Frank. And, Darcy, this is the daughter I was telling you about that does the trick riding." Penny's eyes raised to Blakely's. "Darcy loves horses."

Blakely grinned. She wasn't the only girl through the years that had come to their house and been horse crazy. There had been a lot of them. She didn't have any trouble at all spending time in the ring with those girls. She'd actually given a lot of them horseback riding lessons. There were three who had been adopted close enough that their parents still brought them for lessons from Blakely. She always gave those kids lessons for free.

She didn't have a whole big ton of talents, like Ruby, her sister who was a surgeon and could operate on children and forgo her doctor's fees, and often did. Her brother Denver and his wife, Natalie, donated fruit and Christmas trees to needy families.

Blakely didn't have anything like that she could do, and sometimes, it bothered her. Like she wanted a bigger purpose. But having a girl fall in love with horses and being able to nurture that love, she told herself that it kept them out of trouble and gave those girls purposes and smiles.

Darcy's eyes had lit up when Miss Penny had told her about Blakely.

"You guys want to come over to the barns? I saw Dante there earlier." She didn't add that she hoped she didn't see him again. Although, with the way Frank looked, she probably wouldn't have any choice but to introduce him. Maybe she could pawn him off on Martin and have her friend do it. She wouldn't even feel guilty about it, since Frank was sure to have a great time with Martin, Dante or no Dante. "I think there's a litter of piglets that were just born a couple of days ago. They're really sweet. If Mr. Bill is around, he might let us hold one."

As long as they didn't make it squeal. The mama pig could get pretty upset if one of her babies sounded like it was in distress.

The kids nodded eagerly and came around the table.

They both seemed like they were a little bit too big to hold hands, although Blakely would prefer holding hands and taking them along that way. She'd never lost a kid, but her brother Shawn had once. They'd found the lost child down by the creek, getting ready to start wading.

It wouldn't have been too bad, if it hadn't rained for the three straight days and nights before, and the creek was swollen and muddy and angry, and the kid was almost certain to have drowned.

It shook Shawn pretty bad, but after the initial scare, their parents had been very understanding about it. Everyone in the search party had given examples of when they'd lost their children, even if it was something as simple as the department store parking lot or even one lady lost her kid in her own house.

The kid had been hiding under their bed, but the room was so messy she hadn't found him the three times she looked and ended up calling 911, and the whole neighborhood had been searching. Finally, the kid had fallen asleep. He'd been pouting under their bed.

They'd found all that out when he'd woken up, hungry, and come out from under the bed.

That lady had felt like an idiot.

When the kids had settled in, one on either side of her, Blakely turned. "This way. We'll see the piglets first, and then we'll go to the horses."

"What about Dante? When do I get to see him?"

"We'll keep an eye out for him. I'm really not sure where he is. But I bet he'll pop up somewhere." The festival wasn't that big.

The day had started to get warm, with the brilliant blue sky containing just a few white puffy clouds. There was enough breeze to whip tablecloths off tables but not enough to make it feel cool. It raised a little dust though.

"So, what do you guys like to do?" Blakely asked, to make conversation as they made their way to the animal barn. Despite the calendar, it was decorated in greenery and lights with a big red bow over the door entrance, which was flanked by two super large candy canes.

"I like horses," Darcy said, her voice holding a hint of shyness but also eagerness.

"And I like football. But I wouldn't mind riding a horse as long as it goes fast," Frank said, eagerly peering inside the dim interior of the barn as they reached the entrance.

Clear out the end, Blakely was just able to make out Martin and a couple other guys putting makeshift pens together and shaking bedding in them.

The piglets were at this end, tucked in the corner in one of the permanent pens.

Mr. Bill wasn't around, so they just stood at the gate and looked.

"They're cute," Darcy said, sounding surprised. Like she hadn't really thought that pigs could be cute.

"Babies are always cute. But I don't think there's too many animals that are cuter than a baby pig."

"They look funny," Frank said.

"Hey, Blakely, bring the kids down here. They can pet these bunnies," Martin called, his voice echoing down the tunnel-like interior of the barn.

"Want to pet some bunnies, guys?" Both of the kids were kind of looking down the barn like they weren't sure whether they could trust the man who spoke. "That's Mr. Martin, and he's my best friend."

"You mean he's your boyfriend," Frank said in a kind of taunting voice, reminiscent of middle school, which was probably about his age.

"No. I mean my best friend. He's not my boyfriend, never has been." *And never will be*, she added to herself, but for some reason, she didn't say it out loud. It was a thought she'd always had, but somehow today, or lately, it just didn't feel right anymore.

She was just about to reach Martin, with the kids on either side of her, when she saw Dante coming around the corner of the barn.

Maybe she was mistaken, but it seemed like his eyes landed on her and lit up, his stride lengthening and speeding up.

"Martin?" she said, her voice holding a note of panic that even she could hear.

He recognized it immediately, and his head popped up. She nodded at Dante, and Martin looked in that direction. Immediately, he understood the situation. "Hey, kids, come on over here. Peggy said you could pet her bunny."

The kids stared with open mouths at the cute-looking animal.

"This is Darcy. This is Frank," Blakely said in rushed tones. "I'll be right back." *After he leaves*, she mouthed to Martin, who understood her perfectly.

She turned on her toes and practically sprinted to the makeshift stalls they had set up, twisting to the other side of the loft ladder and scrambling up.

She made it to the top, intending to peek over the side and watch for Dante to leave.

It was immature of her to run, but in her experience, when her parents started trying to pair people up, they succeeded.

Maybe if you wanted a football player, you'd be more interested.

That wasn't true, and she knew it. In the back of her head, she'd been thinking all along that he just didn't compare to Martin. Didn't have the rough hands, the easygoing walk, the natural grin, and he didn't know her inside out and upside down and could finish her sentences for her.

She didn't want someone who was so stuck on himself, who couldn't work, who didn't make her laugh...who wasn't Martin.

She was judging him harshly, and she castigated herself for it.

Crawling over, she came to the end of the stack of hay bales that were probably there from last year and just about jumped out of her skin to see her sister, Journee, sitting there writing something in a notebook.

"Holy smokes. You scared me to death." She sat back on her haunches and glared at her sister. "What are you doing here?"

"It's obvious, isn't it?" Journee said, closing the notebook as though she were afraid Blakely would be looking over her shoulder.

"No?" Blakely said.

"What are you doing up here?" Journee asked, effectively changing the subject with the odd look she gave Blakely, which immediately put her on the defensive.

"I'm hiding from him." Blakely jerked her chin in the direction of the guys. They were too far under the edge of the loft for Journee to see them, but their voices carried up clearly.

"You're hiding from Martin?" Journee asked, her face scrunched up, and her head tilted.

"No, silly." Although that was who had been speaking. "From the football player."

Journee's lips canted up, and she grinned knowingly.

Blakely rolled over to the edge of the loft, peering down.

She was hiding from the ballplayer, sure, but she couldn't just neglect her responsibility to the children. Although Martin would take care of them, and she was fine with that as long as the children were. She and Martin had taken care of her parents' different foster children plenty of times. Usually together though.

She hated ditching him like she had, but she knew he would understand. The football player was not for her.

She made it to the edge and lifted her head slowly and carefully, just wanting to make sure that Martin and the children were okay.

They looked good. Martin had given Frank a hammer and a nail, and he was working on trying to get it nailed into a two-by-four that lay on the ground.

Blakely was pretty sure the nail didn't need to go into the board.

Martin was just giving the kid something to do to make him feel important.

Martin was so good with children.

He had gone down on one knee, with the bunny in his hand, and Darcy ran her hand over the soft fur with wonder in her eyes.

Content that the children were doing good and that Martin wasn't overwhelmed, Blakely gathered herself to push back, but as she did, Martin's head lifted up, and their eyes met.

Immediately, his eyes crinkled with humor at her situation, and for some reason, her heart started beating hard, thundering in her chest like she'd run a mile.

Something odd tingled there too, like a low-voltage buzz of electricity, just humming under her skin.

Even odder to her was that she didn't want to take her eyes away.

She might have lain there staring into Martin's eyes forever, but movement out of the corner of her eye made her turn her head.

Chapter Twelve

The football player was staring at her.

Blakely scrambled back, dropping her head immediately, knowing it was too late.

She was an idiot.

"I take it from the way you're acting that someone saw you," Journee said, muted humor in her voice.

"Yeah. Martin was laughing at me, and the football player happened to look up. And there I was." She sat up and brushed her front off, crossing her legs and giving her sister a sincere look. Leaning forward, she put her hand on her knee. "I did need to talk to you. And it looks like you have some time?"

Journee laughed a little and rolled her eyes. "You're up here. You might as well tell me whatever it was that you wanted to tell me."

"I need advice."

"I thought the younger sister was supposed to get advice from the older sister?"

"Forget all that. This is important."

"What do you need?"

Blakely explained about the kissing contest. "But you can see that Martin and I don't want to win."

"Yeah. Whoever wins gets badgered constantly to kiss for the next hundred years at least. Unless you break up and marry other people, and then you still might get begged to kiss. There are no guarantees in a small town."

"Exactly. So Martin and I don't want to win. But neither one of us has ever watched the kissing contest."

"You're missing out. You can learn a lot of things from the kissing contest."

"Well, I guess we'll get to learn this year, but we need to know, what do winners do? We need to make sure we don't do that."

Journee eyed her. Blakely wasn't sure what to make of that look. It was almost like Journee was thinking the kissing contest was going to be more than what Blakely intended it to be somehow.

Blakely tapped her fingers on her leg, waiting. Finally, she couldn't stand the silence of her sister any longer. "I was thinking if we just act awkward. You know, like turn our heads the same way, miss our mouths, giggle... What else?"

"You haven't kissed too many people, have you?"

"That has nothing to do with this."

"I'm not saying that's a bad thing, I'm just saying awkwardness is kinda cute in a first kiss especially. The audience will love it, and the judges will score high. I mean, it's not like a super romantic Hollywood kiss, but it's perfect for small towns. Awkwardness, giggling, fumbling a little. People love it."

That was the opposite of everything Blakely had been thinking. She was glad she'd asked. Her mind was already adjusting their potential strategy. "Okay. So we have to pretend that we're old hands at kissing." At the thought of kissing Martin, her stomach cramped in a not-unpleasurable kind of way, and her hands tingled. "That might be hard."

"That's what I was thinking. No one's gonna believe that you and

Martin all the sudden want to kiss each other, and have been for a long time, unless you guys act like you're already together."

"You think we should? Should we be like holding hands or something so people think that we're actually a couple? Because I can kinda see your point. Kissing probably gets boring after you've been with someone for a while."

"Maybe you should spend a little less time with your horses and a little more time figuring out how to live life," Journee said, shoving her pencil down the spiral of her notebook, closing it, and setting it aside.

"You're a good one to talk. Other than Alex, who doesn't really count, you've never had a boyfriend."

"Maybe Alex was enough."

But the dreamy look on Journee's face told a different story. Blakely narrowed her eyes suspiciously, moving to the notebook and then back to Journee. Her parents had been talking for a while about the pen pal program at the church. For a little bit, Blakely had written to four different people.

But it was snail mail, which people didn't really have the patience for anymore. All of her pen pals had puttered out.

Still, Blakely couldn't bring herself to say anything. Journee had been deeply hurt by Alex. The whole town knew it.

She was so sweet, with a big heart that was willing to help anyone, and often did. Nursing was perfect for her, except she did have a tendency to have her head in the clouds like she did right now.

Still, Blakely felt extremely protective of her younger sister and figured that's the way the entire town felt.

Alex most likely would not be welcome back, and anyone else who tried to hurt Journee would face the wrath of Mistletoe.

On the one hand, Blakely figured that would be pretty nice. On the other, she liked being thought of as someone who could take care of herself. She supposed, with the trick riding she did, she was looked at as being pretty fearless.

Maybe in trick riding she was. She definitely could push the envelope, riding fast, pushing hard, doing tricks that were more than a little dangerous, and she paid the price for that more than once by getting hurt. Somehow though, physical hurt didn't scare her.

Issues of the heart? That was a little different.

Journee was right; she had her head in her horses so much, through so much of her life, that she really had never learned how to handle things.

Case in point, she was up here in the hayloft hiding from the man she thought her parents were trying to set her up with, instead of going up to him, like a mature almost thirty-year-old would do, and saying she wasn't interested.

She supposed that said a lot about Martin that he was willing to put up with her. And she'd never even realized how much her emotional immaturity probably affected him.

Now that her eyes were open to it though, she could be more aware and, hopefully, take advantage of him less.

If that's what she did indeed do.

Although, the football player had changed things a little. She didn't usually hide out.

"I'll give you that," she finally said. Her sister said Alex had been enough, and even though she looked a little dreamy, like she might be writing to someone who was slightly more than a friend, Blakely wasn't going to call her on it. "The kissing contest is tomorrow. Do you think we have enough time to act like we're a couple?"

"Will Martin even go along with it?"

Blakely bit her lip and twisted a straw stem in her hand. "I think so. Our parents are actually pushing Krissy at him, and he and I have an agreement. I think he'd be willing to do this to make it look legit."

"He helps you, and you help him?" Journee said, and there might have been just a trace of envy in her voice. Like she wished she had a best friend who would do the same for her.

"I'm pretty blessed to have Martin," Blakely said, responding to the tone of her voice and not the words.

"You are. I think maybe neither one of you know exactly what you have," she said thoughtfully, running her finger down the spirals of her notebook and not looking at Blakely while she said it.

"You might be right about that." She'd been having those thoughts lately about how blessed she'd been to have a best friend like Martin. A friendship like theirs wasn't an everyday occurrence. "I'm pretty sure he'll go along with it. Do you think it will work?" That was where Blakely was stumbling. Would people believe they were together if they were just together for a day?

"I don't think you need to be obvious about it. Just let him put his arm around you. The rumor mill will pick it up and take it from there. You know how rumors travel in a small town. All you and Martin need to do is hold hands, and the whole town's going to have you married by next Friday."

Blakely grunted. "True."

"I know."

"Now about the kind of kiss that we need to have. You said awkward was a winning attribute. What's a losing attribute?"

"Disinterest?" Journee said, scrunching her brows up, her finger going to her cheek thoughtfully. "Or, I don't know, there's just no spark. Boring. Like you've done it a million times and you don't really care about the person you're kissing. I think those kisses are the ones that are forgettable and that nobody votes for."

"Nobody votes for? I thought there were judges?"

"There are, but they also get audience participation. It varies from year to year, and the judges' scores are weighted heavily, but typically, they take opinions from the audience. But every year, it's been different. The kissing contest is kind of eccentric, which is another appeal."

"Great. So basically, we don't know exactly what to expect?"

"That's pretty much right. Just know that the audience will have some say in it. And they don't like boring."

"That should be easy. Martin and I are friends. The idea of kissing has never crossed our minds." At least, it hadn't crossed hers until recently, when she'd begun dreaming about it. Which was not something she was going to admit to anyone, ever. "We should be able to do boring and uninspired. Although, it'll be really hard to make it look like we've done it a million times before. And I care about him, so I might have to try to pretend that I don't."

"There's a difference between caring about someone as a friend and caring about someone to the point where you don't want to take your lips off his," Journee said, almost sounding wise.

"You're my little sister. You're really not supposed to know more about this than I do."

"That's not my fault. Maybe you should have spent more of your teenaged years doing what everyone else was doing and a little less time immersed in your horses."

Blakely couldn't disagree with the fact that she was light-years behind everyone else socially. She'd already figured she was emotionally stunted from focusing on her horses. She was probably socially stunted too. She'd lived and breathed horses all of her life. Working with Martin on the ranch hadn't really done much to help her get out.

"I think it might be too late for me."

"You're really going to a lot of effort to try to avoid that football player. Is he that bad?"

Blakely crossed her arms over her chest and looked away. She had to be honest. "He's probably not that bad. I just don't know. I don't want to know. I guess that shows that I'm shallow and pathetic."

"A little probably."

"Thanks."

"You want the truth. You're judging him based on what he does for a living. Or what he looks like. And that's wrong. You know that."

"I know."

"But don't be too hard on yourself. This is just an area where you don't do very well. And you have to do better. But there's no one that has a bigger heart than you do. You're always putting other people ahead of yourself. Look at the kids that you give lessons to without charging. And I did hear that a certain person was out at Martin's ranch, and you were showing your secret trick to her. Your competition. And you are helping her. That says a lot about your character. No one expects you to be perfect."

"She's my competition, true, but she's kind of a friend as well."

"She's not nearly as good a friend to you as you are to her. And you don't have to sugarcoat that. Because it's true. There aren't a lot of people who would have done what you did. Helped her, and she's giving you nothing in return. Nothing besides telling everyone how wonderful your best friend is and letting everyone know that she's got her eye on him." Journee kind of gave Blakely a calculating look. Blakely wasn't sure what it meant, but she did know her lungs tightened at the idea that Journee knew Erin had her eye on Martin.

"Martin would never go for her."

Journee just raised her brows while Blakely tried not to squirm. She supposed someone would be snatching Martin up, especially if he were done on the rodeo circuit.

"You think Martin likes her?" she asked hesitantly, unsure why the idea sat so badly with her and trying to remember what, exactly, Martin had said. Maybe he'd wanted to go help her but had stayed with Blakely because he felt guilty or something.

Journee lifted a shoulder. "You know better than I do."

Blakely sat for a bit and stared at her lap, thinking. She did know Martin pretty well, as well as he knew her, which was better than anyone in the world. But she really didn't know whether or not he would like Erin.

"Do you think I'm holding him back?" she asked softly. Maybe he would have gone to Erin and helped her, except he was tied down with Blakely.

She hadn't even considered that maybe she was being selfish.

Although, she supposed she just assumed it was one of the

things that they did for each other, like she worked far harder on his ranch than what she needed to in order to pay for boarding her horses and giving riding lessons there.

She'd given way more time than she'd needed to. But she'd never kept track.

Friends didn't. At least not in her book.

She didn't have a I-do-this-for-you-you-do-this-for-me kind of friendship. Just if she had an opportunity to do something for Martin, she did it. There was no scoreboard.

It was just friendship.

"No," Journee said. "Martin isn't the kind of person who's gonna sit around and let someone walk all over him while he secretly pines away for something else. If he wants Erin, he'll go get her. You don't need to worry about that."

The thought clarified in her head, and she knew it to be true. Martin would do anything for her, but if he wanted Erin, he wouldn't hide that from Blakely.

"Is there something you think I need to worry about?" Blakely asked, just because Journee's statements seemed to be open-ended.

"I think you have to answer that question," Journee said enigmatically. "Now, there is something that I can do for you, since you're my older sister, and I love you."

"What's that?" Blakely asked, a little suspicious at Journee's tone.

"I can get that football player away from you. I think, most of the time, Mom and Dad are right, but if they're trying to match you up with him, they're definitely missing the mark on that one. I can make it so that you don't need to worry about him."

"I wouldn't ask you to do that."

"I know. You didn't ask. I offered. You won't have to worry about running from him." Journee lifted a brow, indicating Blakely's position in the hayloft.

"I'm immature and stupid. We've already figured that out."

"No. You just don't have any experience in matters of the heart,"

Journee said, setting her notebook aside and rising gracefully, a little smile on her face. "And that's not necessarily a bad thing. You don't have to know how to handle every man in the world. You just have to be faithful to one."

"You can't be faithful if you can't catch him."

"Maybe it's not a matter of catching, maybe it's a matter of being caught."

"He's not exactly been chasing me around."

"The football player?"

"He's obviously not a good match for me."

Journee nodded thoughtfully. "Usually, our parents have much better insight. I can hardly believe..." Absentmindedly, Journee fixed her shirt and brushed the hay off her pants, her face still pulled together in puzzled contemplation.

"Maybe they're just off their game."

"They can't be too far off. They just helped West and Poppy a few months ago."

"True." Blakely stood with Journee, following her to the loft ladder. "I guess they can't be right all the time. Just most of it."

Journee nodded. "They've definitely given me some good advice over the years. You'd be wise to listen to them. But I do agree with you on this. The ballplayer...he's not for you."

"Maybe he's for you."

Journee shook her head. "No." A little smile played at the corners of her mouth. "But I think we could probably be friends."

She was two rungs down before she looked up at Blakely. "You stay here until I get him to take me to see the sheep with the triplets. I think they're two sheds down, and that should be far enough so that you can grab Martin and take the kids and do something."

"Thank you."

She wasn't sure if Martin was finished with what he was doing, but it would at least give her time to get the kids and go to the horse barn. She'd be in her element there.

"Just avoid the horse barn. And that's where I'll stay." It wouldn't be hard to get Darcy there, but Frank might be another story. Although he seemed interested in a ride.

Maybe now would be a good time for Martin and her to establish their "relationship."

With that thought in mind, she put her foot on the top rung of the ladder and started down.

Chapter Thirteen

artin straightened, putting the rabbit back in its pen.
"This is a pretty hands-on festival. I like it,"
Dante said from behind him.

Dante had turned out to be a nice guy. Martin understood Blakely's aversion, for the most part. He did seem kind of intimidating, and her parents had a way of finagling things around.

Blakely wasn't cut out to be a ballplayer's girl. And she knew it, even if she couldn't articulate it quite that way.

"It's always been like that. I think it's good for the kids. So many things they don't usually get to see and experience, and it's all here at the Mistletoe Christmas festival," Martin said, turning to Dante. Frank stood almost glued to his side, stars in his eyes and hero worship all over his face.

Darcy was far less impressed, but she had been pretty excited about the rabbit.

"Blakely will be back soon, and then you'll get to see the horses." Darcy's eyes lit up at his words.

"She was up in the loft. Almost like she was hiding from

someone. She's...not quite all there?" Dante asked, his voice lowering, his finger pointing in the general direction of his head.

"Yeah," Martin said, hiding his smirk. "Pretty much." Blakely could thank him later.

He turned his head to see Journee hopping off the loft ladder and walking over. "This is her sister, Journee. She's normal," Martin added, striving to keep any trace of humor out of his tone.

Blakely seemed so confident and sure of herself when she was performing.

Most people didn't realize that she hid a personality that wasn't nearly so brave. She'd never practiced being around people, even in high school. So wrapped up in her horses.

He was probably an enabler, because he'd run interference for her for years. He was much better at the social end of things, and she was better on the animal side. She was even better with cattle than he was.

"I see," Dante said, sounding for all the world like he didn't. His eyes were glued on Journee, and he had some weird expression on his face. Odd.

Martin turned again, wondering if Journee had some kind of rash or something that would explain Dante's look.

But he didn't get a chance to examine her too closely, because Blakely jumped off the loft ladder and came running over.

That wasn't too unusual. Once Blakely got something in her head, she usually went full steam with it. *Why walk when you can run* could be her life's motto.

She didn't stop beside him but barreled into him, throwing her arms around him. He forgot all about Dante and Journee as he caught Blakely against him, feeling the strong lines of her body, feeling her heat, and breathing in her woman's scent, sort of sweet but mostly wild. It did some crazy things to his head and his heart— both of them felt dizzy and off-kilter. By the time he'd fought off the crazy desire to pull her close and drop his lips to the line of her jaw and remembered about Dante and Journee, they were gone.

Thankfully, the men were unloading a truck full of goats, and the children stood at the temporary barrier, watching with rapt attention.

"This is new," he breathed, softer and warmer than he intended.

Definitely new and definitely not unpleasant.

"Is it okay?" Blakely said, her voice husky and slightly out of breath. "Journee said we probably ought to act like we're a couple, if we wanted people to believe we're boring for the kissing contest."

Something sharp and hard seemed to sink into his middle. Disappointment maybe?

It wasn't real. She was just pretending.

It had felt real to him.

A deep breath pushed the feeling away, and he tightened his arms. "'Course it is. Anything for the kissing contest."

"We need to lose. We have to be convincing."

"I see. So we're supposed to be pretending to actually be a couple?" Somehow, his voice sounded normal, despite the turmoil in his chest. There was no doubt this was not good for him. He was definitely starting to feel more than friendly feelings for his best friend. He was starting to step into dangerous territory.

Even though the idea of pretending to be a couple was not repugnant. Not at all.

"Is that okay?" she whispered in his ear, sounding worried.

He pulled back, seeing Frank and Darcy still standing watching the goats, and if he wasn't mistaken, they were discussing the possibility of them getting a goat.

"Martin?" Blakely sounded concerned, her normally joyful expression twisted into concern.

"It's fine. I'm sorry. I was just thinking."

"I get it. This could ruin everything. I don't want to make things awkward between us."

"That's true. Our friendship means more to me than anything. If this stupid kissing contest or anything else is going to screw it up, we just flat-out need to not do it rather than take a chance on messing up the best relationship I've ever had."

"Me too. I appreciate you more than I can tell you. You've always been there for me, and I feel so comfortable with you, but I know there are things we can do that could ruin everything."

"I absolutely think you're right. We need to be careful." They weren't pressed against each other, but her arms were still locked around his neck, and his were still on her waist. Hard, muscular, solid, as befitted someone who was as active and athletic as she was.

She probably didn't realize it, but her fingers played with the hair that curled at the nape of his neck. He should have gotten it cut a long time ago, but he hadn't, and he loved what she was doing. He couldn't admit it though, couldn't tell her, but also couldn't ask her not to stop. That was definitely one of those things that would make their friendship weird.

Thankfully she didn't stop, and she stepped a little closer. "Journee said—"

"I know. And that's fine. We just need to be careful." Maybe it was just him struggling with feelings that had no business in friendship. Just him that all of the sudden realized that having Blakely in his arms was better than having her beside him. That he wanted, maybe craved, a lot more than her friendship.

If he were smart, he'd probably back out of the kissing contest.

"I was able to get some great info from Journee on the kind of kiss we need in order to lose."

"Are you taking me to see the horses?" Darcy asked, looking up at both of them.

Immediately, Blakely's face flowed into a grin, and she stepped back, her arms dropping.

Martin allowed his arms to drop too, although he didn't want to.

"Of course. We can see if Mr. Martin can go with us." She looked up, her eyes asking questions. The other men had finished unloading the goats and disappeared.

"I'm sure I can take some time and we can go hang out with the horses for a bit."

Darcy's face expanded into a beautiful little-girl smile, and even Frank looked happy.

"Thanks, Martin."

Their eyes hooked again. He felt that same odd churning in his chest.

He pushed it aside. Blakely was helping him by being in the contest with him. He was going to do this so they wouldn't win, for Blakely, and it didn't matter what kind of personal sacrifice he had to make. He would do it for his best friend.

As they turned, her hand slipped into his, and he was too shocked to move.

He'd given her a hand up plenty of times, and she'd done the same for him. They'd handed things off to each other, skin brushing skin, and he'd never given it a second thought.

But today? With her hand sliding against his, her fingers curling around, and their palms pressed together, his lungs suddenly wouldn't work, and his heart was far more interested in Blakely's fingers in his than it was in pumping blood to his brain.

He let out a shaky breath and turned and looked down. "Part of our ruse?"

He didn't need to say anything, but he felt like he should, and those were the only words in his brain that were acceptable to let past his lips.

She nodded, and he somehow got the feeling that maybe, maybe she was having a little trouble with this too.

If only. Could she be feeling the same things he was?

He somehow doubted it.

"Am I going to be able to ride a horse?" Darcy's voice came up between them from Blakely's other side.

"You can definitely sit on one. I might be leading it around for you."

"You could do some tricks?" Frank asked, sounding eager.

"I sure will. I have both Candy and Kisses here in the stable, and we'll get one of them out, and I'll do a few things."

"Cool! Can I do some tricks too? Will you teach me?"

"I sure will. They take a lot of time to learn though, so it's not like you'll be doing tricks today. We have to start at the beginning, and I can tell you all the steps we need in order to put a trick together."

Blakely looked down at Frank, who didn't seem like he understood.

Martin smiled to himself. He understood exactly what Frank was thinking. He liked to have everything immediately as well. Seemed like a typical male thing. Although, as he aged, it got easier to wait. For some things anyway.

"I think the best way I can explain it," Blakely started, "is doing tricks on horses is kind of like playing a game of football. You don't start out on the first day of practice putting pads and uniforms and helmets on and running plays. Right?"

Frank nodded, maybe having played peewee football or something else similar. He definitely had understanding in his eyes.

"Trick riding is the same way. There's a foundation that has to be built before you can use that foundation to go further and do more. Just like you have to run and lift weights and get in shape, and then you run drills, study patterns, and learn techniques before you actually line up against an opposing team."

"I get it. The first part of football practice is boring, because all we do is run and get tired, and I hate it."

"That's what makes you strong. That's what's going to make you into a good player. The better you can do the basics, the more solid your foundation is when you try to do more."

Frank didn't seem like he understood all of that, although he definitely understood about not starting out with trick riding. Martin figured it would take him a few years before he really appreciated the idea of a solid foundation.

Blakely's hand squeezed his, and he squeezed back. Funny that he should think about a solid foundation.

He never really thought about what it took to make marriage work, or even a relationship, really, but he could see that the exact same things Blakely had been just telling Frank were true in a marriage and in a relationship between two people. A solid friendship. Trust. Loyalty. Sacrifice. Having proved oneself during trials and hardships. Those were the things that laid down a solid foundation for a lifetime commitment.

He shook his head. He never thought about junk like that.

Maybe you should.

He wanted to have a solid marriage like his parents did. He supposed that meant taking the time to figure out what it entailed, because his mom wasn't the only one who worked on her marriage. His dad had made sure that he was a fun guy to get and be married to.

That wasn't something he normally thought about, but it was almost as though with the feelings that Blakely had awakened, his thoughts had been shifted too.

There didn't seem to be any putting them back to sleep.

Blakely was chatting with Darcy about horse behavior, and he risked a glance in her direction.

How would she feel about taking another step and furthering their relationship? Everything was clicking into place for him, but maybe he was the only one.

It was hard for him to figure out any scenario in his mind where he could ask her without tipping his hand and making everything awkward.

He was definitely thinking about things he'd never thought about before. That was for sure.

When they came around the corner, Blakely jerked, and her step hesitated.

Then her chin went up, her shoulders back, her chest out, and she continued on like nothing was wrong.

But Erin was in the arena, with Peaches, and as they watched, she flew ahead at full speed before pulling Peaches into a sliding stop, apparently attempting the trick that Blakely had just taught her a couple of days ago.

But she wasn't doing it right, because she barely made it halfway around and landed in the dirt on her shoulder.

From the way her outfit looked, that wasn't the first time she'd landed in the dirt.

Martin didn't laugh at her. He didn't believe in enjoying another person's bad luck, but he was tempted to, just for Blakely's sake. That had to look good to her. Knowing that Blakely had given Erin all the secrets of her trick, and she hadn't been able to figure it out.

Especially now that Blakely was back in the competition.

That had to give her confidence.

"Did she mean to do that?" Frank asked. Maybe he was having second thoughts about being a trick rider if it involved landing on your head in the dirt.

"That happens sometimes. Being a trick rider is fun, but there's a lot of pain involved," Blakely said matter-of-factly.

Martin agreed with her. He didn't see any point in lying to the kid. If he was going to be good at anything, there was going to be pain involved. Sacrifice. And a lot of perseverance.

"Is that the kind of tricks you do?" Darcy asked, her eyes wide open.

"Miss Blakely actually just taught Erin that trick."

"Really? That's your trick?" Darcy asked, her voice dripping with amazement.

"Actually, yeah. I made that trick up."

"Next week, Miss Blakely and Miss Erin will be competing. It's good for Miss Blakely if Miss Erin doesn't catch on."

Blakely looked at him, half smiling, half resignation. "It's good for me, but I can't not help. It wouldn't be right."

"That whole do unto others thing?" Martin asked, understanding immediately.

She nodded, and her hand slid out of his. She slipped between the fence rails and walked over. By that time, Erin was up and brushing herself off.

Both of the kids grabbed a hold of the fence and stuck their heads in between the slats, watching.

"Blakely. I wasn't expecting to see you."

Martin almost rolled his eyes. Where else would Blakely be the day before Mistletoe's annual Christmas festival? Erin knew for a fact she'd be here. She probably also knew she was having trouble with her trick and that Blakely would probably help her.

Erin was definitely taking advantage of Blakely, and Martin figured that most people in the world would say that Blakely had every right to snub her and walk away.

But she wouldn't be the girl he knew, she wouldn't be his best friend, if that's the way she acted.

She didn't let him down.

Blakely said, "I saw you start. And you're doing great through the gallop. But what happens is just before you pulled Peaches to a stop, you tensed up. You gotta stay loose. It's the only way the trick works."

Erin listened to Blakely, hanging on her every word like it was gospel. "It's such a little thing, but that explains why I was doing the trick just fine when you were working with me before. I think you're right. I can see how I've changed since then now that you said it. I'm anticipating the stop and tensing up."

"Probably because you landed on your head so many times your body just automatically anticipates that pain. I had to work through that too."

Erin's eyes widened. "How long did it take you?"

Blakely had turned enough that he could see she smiled. Probably finding it humorous that Erin was being so transparent. Her question could have been phrased, "Will I have the bugs worked out in time for the competition?"

"I probably did the trick a hundred times before I landed consistently on my feet. But I didn't have anyone telling me what I was doing wrong. I had a bunch of things I tried before I realized I needed to be loose. You know now exactly what you need to work on."

Darcy and Frank stood with Martin for more than an hour watching Blakely, who eventually went and saddled up Candy and Kisses.

Martin had led Kisses around with Darcy first and then Frank in the saddle, giving them the rides they'd been promised. But neither of them cared too much that the rides were short, because they were too interested in watching the trick riding in the ring and Erin as she worked on the trick. Both of them were enraptured. When Miss Penny finally came over to grab them and take them home to feed them, neither one of them wanted to go.

"I know Blakely will give them lessons on the ranch," Martin said.

Miss Penny nodded. But then her face clouded. "She might not be around in order to do that. And with the festival this weekend, we probably won't have time to make it out."

"I know Blakely will figure something out. Even if she does make the team, there'll be a week or two before she'd have to leave."

"You're right. However it works out, God knows. He's in control."

Martin nodded. He believed that too. But it seemed kind of odd timing that he'd all the sudden realized that maybe he was thinking about Blakely as more than a friend, and she was thinking about leaving for up to three years.

This doesn't seem like perfect timing, Lord.

Maybe the perfect timing was that Blakely didn't feel the same, and he would have three years to get over any stupid things he ended up doing between now and when she left.

Because she would be leaving. Unless some fluke thing happened like it had at the last competition, she'd be going, because she really was the best trick rider in the country. Hands down.

And as her best friend, Martin knew that when she won the

competition, he needed to be happy for her. No matter how hard it was for him.

Chapter Fourteen

It was late when Martin and Blakely returned to the ranch and unloaded Candy and Kisses from the horse trailer, tucking them into their stalls.

Blakely could have left them at the festival grounds, but although Mistletoe was a small town and nothing probably would happen to them, they were too valuable to her to leave them there without her staying with them.

Not that she thought anyone would steal them, but there was the rabbit and chicken incident, with their cages having been opened.

She didn't think anyone would actually hurt her horses on purpose, but she didn't want to chance it.

After Martin, Candy and Kisses were her best friends.

"You know you didn't have to help me," she said as she closed Candy's stall door and latched it.

"I know. There are lots of times when you didn't have to help me either."

"Oh? We're keeping track now?"

"I'm not. Only you. That's okay. You owe me, and I'm okay with that."

"Really?" She tilted her head down and gave him a look. "Pretty sure you know better."

"Pretty sure I don't." He grinned.

"All right. You're right. I owe you, and I'll never be able to repay you for all of the things you've done for me. There. Beat that." She grinned as she started walking toward the door.

He fell into step beside her. "I can't. Because with all the work that you've done on the ranch, how you've helped me hold it together through the drought seven years ago, when you loaned me every last penny you had so I could buy hay to get the stock through the winter. Where you sat up with me at night, trying to figure out how we could stretch and pull and twist and turn to make ends meet... Honestly, I could never repay you. The ranch should be half yours."

Blakely swallowed. She thought their conversation would be light and goofy. She hadn't meant for him to get serious.

"I think your wife wouldn't be real happy about that." It was a comment she would have made flippantly a million times before, except this time she actually thought about it.

Martin with a wife.

A wife that wasn't her.

She hadn't had the best day. It had been hard to show Erin the trick again and coach her through it, knowing that she was most likely going to beat her out for the spot on the trick riding team if she mastered it and yet knowing that what she was doing was exactly what she wanted to do, even if it was hard and even if it hurt. Even if it took away from her dream. Because she didn't want to realize her dreams only because she hadn't helped someone else.

It didn't make sense.

'Course, it didn't make sense to be helping her competition, either. She should be working her butt off to win, not helping the competition get better.

No one in the world would think she should do what she did.

Except Martin.

What if Erin wanted Martin?

If Erin asked her to help her catch Martin's eye, would she do that too?

"Looks like you're thinking about a problem. Need some help?"

She shook her head, not liking the automatic answer that her mind had for that question. She did want to be that kind of a person.

"No. Just me trying to be selfish when I know I shouldn't be."

"Because you're helping Erin? I was so proud of you. You have no idea what it's like to have a friend that's so selfless. Gives me a good feeling right here." He tapped his chest.

The way she'd been feeling about him lately, that's exactly where she wanted him to have his feelings, but pride wasn't really what she was going for.

"No. Not really. It was easier today than it was the first time."

"Each time you do something right, something hard, it gets easier. I suppose that's true."

"Yeah. It is. I think. Although, I don't know if I'll ever do it without a little pain. You know, giving up what you want and basically handing it to someone else. It's hard."

He put a hand on her shoulder and shook it just a little. "I love that you do the hard thing. That didn't just start today. Or this week. The whole time we've been friends, you've never been afraid to take the hard road."

She looked down, appreciating his words, but... "There are so many things I want to be better at. Like today. When I ran away from Dante. Just the thoughts I've had about him haven't been nice at all. I've been a real brat in my head. I'm just so socially inept, it's ridiculous. I mean, come on, what kind of person hides in the hayloft because they're afraid that some guy might hit on them?"

"I think we might be surprised. That's probably not as uncommon as we think."

She gave him a baleful look. "You're not making me feel any better. You know, one of a kind."

"Sure. You're one of a kind, but not in that area."

He lapsed into silence. She didn't say anything. Not really feeling better, but not feeling worse. She supposed, if she were perfect, life would be boring. "It's probably always good to have a struggle, right? Gives us something to work on."

"Not to change the subject, but something to work on reminded me, you were in the hayloft with Journee, and you said you're going to ask her about the kissing contest. What did she say?" Martin flinched, not hugely, but just a little like a wince, as he said it, and it made her feel like he really didn't want to do the kissing contest.

She supposed, in a way, she agreed with him. She didn't want to do it, but it was more because she didn't want to lose her best friend or do something stupid. Would he be able to tell she was attracted to him if she couldn't quit kissing him?

"What? You afraid to tell me?" He shoved a hand in his pocket, and slowly, the other hand moved from her shoulder.

Maybe it was her imagination, but it seemed to run down her arm with his fingertips just lightly trailing before he shoved that hand in his other pocket and leaned his shoulder up against the barn post.

"I mean, come on. It can't be that hard, right? If we want to lose, we'll just be awkward and look like we don't know what we're doing. Maybe I can miss your mouth or something."

She narrowed her eyes at him. "Maybe you can say that in a tone that doesn't imply that that's an impossibility."

"Busted." He grinned, and she stared at the cleft in his chin. Familiar and yet not.

She'd seen it pretty much every day of her life for years and years. But she hadn't really thought anything about it. Maybe she'd taken its presence for granted. Or the presence of the person on whom it was attached.

No, she didn't think she'd ever really taken Martin for granted, necessarily.

Maybe she'd taken for granted the idea that they would always be friends.

A wife would complicate things.

If you leave for three years chasing your dreams, that would complicate things too.

She wasn't sure where that thought came from, but it was true.

She brushed her hands down the front of her jeans, knowing she was dusty and dirty and needed to shower. And suddenly, wanting one, wanting to be clean and not to smell like horses. Not when she was standing in front of Martin.

That was definitely new.

"Actually, Journee said that awkward kisses are crowd favorites. She suggested not looking awkward."

"Really? Why?" Martin's tone implied he really had no clue. "Come on, guys are supposed to have it all together, aren't we? I mean, I get the impression that women think that we're supposed to be perfect at romance, always have the right thing to say, always look tough and rugged but smell like spicy woods and never like manure or sweat. We should have six-pack abs, or eight-pack if possible, no bald spots, and God forbid you have a weak chin. Oh, we're supposed to be perfect kissers. How can you win a kissing contest with an awkward kiss?"

"Wow. I had no idea there was so much bitterness in there." She pointed at his chest, poking it.

He grabbed her finger, but instead of letting go, he held onto it, just holding her fist in front of him. "No bitterness. But that does seem to be what ladies expect. I mean, you don't, but everyone else does."

"Everyone else?"

"Girls in general." He waved his free hand around. "They're all about what a guy looks like. And just from around..."

She narrowed her eyes. "You've been reading romance novels, haven't you?"

"When do I have time to do that?"

"You have!" Her mouth opened, and she wanted to laugh. "I bet if I go right now, you've got a romance sitting on your bedside table."

"I don't have a bedside table."

"It's not a hard question. Have you or have you not been reading romances?"

He shuffled, kicking at the dirt a little with his cowboy boot, and Blakely couldn't close her mouth to save her life.

"Are they good? Maybe they'd help me?" she said, only partially teasing.

"No. All the heroines in them are pretty much like Erin."

All right. She was able to close her mouth now. But her heart hurt. "I'm not really romance novel material, am I?"

"I don't think any of the heroines in my books help their competition be better. So no, I don't think you qualify."

"They probably all say the right things at the right time too, don't they?"

"Honestly, the standard for heroines in romances is way lower than the standard for heroes."

"Maybe that's because women are supposed to be the ones reading romances?" She couldn't stop her lip from hitching up, and he looked abashed.

"Maybe. Natalie gave one to me in church the other week; she said maybe I could use it."

"Natalie? My sister-in-law?"

He nodded. "I trusted her. It didn't look like it would be anything terrible, so I figured I'd try it. She ended up giving me three more so I could finish the series. I mean, you know, they're predictable. Like I've read four now, and every single time, the guy gets the girl. Nothing new about that. The scenarios are ridiculous, but yeah, since Natalie suggested them, I figured I'd try it."

"The scenarios?"

"Yeah. So much coincidence. And they're sappy. And all about thoughts and feelings. There's not enough action and intrigue."

"You're not a fan?" She couldn't keep the humor out of her voice.

"No. Although, if she gives me a few more, I might keep trying them. Maybe I'll find one that breaks the mold."

"Most likely not. I've heard all those things are required in a romance." She lifted her shoulder. "I wouldn't know. I don't have time to read."

"Maybe you should try. Maybe they'd help to keep you from running from potential suitors."

"He is not a potential suitor. He might be a potential friend. And I have to work on that, but not a suitor." She said that firmly so there was no room for argument.

"I think we started this conversation trying to figure out what kind of kiss we need to do tomorrow to lose. And it's been very difficult to keep you focused on the subject matter at hand." His lips pulled back. "Can I have your undivided attention for just three minutes so we can figure this out? Because I, for one, absolutely do not want to win that contest tomorrow."

"Well, that makes two of us. Surely if we're focused on the goal, the goal of losing, we can manage to do this thing."

"If we work hard, we should succeed. "

"Exactly, if we work together and try our best, there should be no way we win that contest."

"Right. But we need a plan. Because we can't be successful without a plan."

"Agreed. You're absolutely right."

They looked at each other, both of them obviously at a loss.

Finally, Blakely spoke. "She said the kisses that do the worst are the ones that look boring. Like they've done it a million times before. Like there's no spark or fun or any kind of emotion."

"In other words, the perfect kiss in a sterile environment?"

Her brows crinkled. "Um... Maybe?"

"Sorry, didn't mean to break out the big words and leave you in the dust."

"Yeah, keep it to two syllables or less, please. I just ride horses for a living, my brain isn't part of that."

"Very funny. Actually, I really love the way you were able to see Erin ride today. You saw her do the trick one time, and you had it analyzed and were able to pinpoint the exact spot where she needed help. That was pretty impressive. Even more impressive was the fact that you helped her, but still. You're pretty amazing."

His words warmed Blakely. Caused that good feeling in her chest where it heated and expanded and she felt noticed and appreciated.

But it also gave her that tight, guilty feeling.

"Words make me feel good. Like someone noticed my sacrifice. But I don't deserve them."

"You sure do. Everything I said was true."

"I acted right. But my heart just wasn't there. I feel like a hypocrite. Because I almost hate Erin. Not because she's a bad person, or because she deserves my hate. But because I resent her. Resent the fact that she's probably going to beat me because I helped her."

"There's something wrong with that."

"There sure is. When you help someone, when you make a sacrifice like that, you should feel good about it. You should love the person and want the best for them. It shouldn't matter what that means for you. You shouldn't hate them, resent them, and half the time wish you hadn't done anything that you'd done. It takes away all of the good things about what you did and makes it a hypocritical action."

"I don't think so. I mean, you're right in a way. God loves a cheerful giver. He's more concerned about our hearts and reactions. But I think, too, whenever you know what's right, and you do it, even when you don't want to, that counts for something. It counts for more than if it were just something that was easy for you and you didn't even have to think about. You know what I mean? Like the widow who gave her last two mites. If she had more money at home, those two mites wouldn't have been that much. But the fact that she didn't, the fact that she gave everything she had, even though it wasn't much, and she was blessed because of it, it's kind of the same idea that you're giving what you have, knowing what's right and doing it."

"I think maybe you're stretching the example a little."

"I think you're just refusing to see anything good in what you did. Maybe because you know your heart and how wicked it is. But that's not a surprise for the Lord. That our hearts are wicked. He says so clearly in the Bible. But even if our hearts are wicked, we can choose to do the right thing. And while right actions follow right thinking, sometimes right thinking causes right actions."

He had a point. "It's better, even if you don't feel right, to do right."

"Of course. You can't be like, I'm not feeling it so I can't do it. A lot of times when you're not feeling it, it's hard to do right."

"I agree." Her lips pressed down. "Still, although everything makes sense, it's still better to have the right heart, the right attitude, than it is to just go around doing things and having resentment and unkindness festering inside of yourself." She wouldn't say anything was festering exactly, in her, but she knew, while she'd helped Erin, she wasn't completely rooting for her.

"I think that'll come in time. You can't act right and have a wrong heart for long. Either you're going to start acting the way you're thinking, or your thinking is going to come around. I think if you know that your thinking needs to come around, it makes it more likely that it will. Because it's probably something you're working on."

"I sure have." She hadn't gotten anywhere though. It would be nice if God could just see that she'd done something right, if she prayed and asked for the right attitude about it, and bam, she got it. The struggling to want good things to happen out of the good things she'd done felt wrong. It felt like those feelings should just be natural.

But she was tired of thinking about it.

So she changed the subject. "Don't think we're any closer to plotting out a way to lose the contest tomorrow. We keep seeming to get sidetracked."

She dug her boot toe into the floor. This subject wasn't much better than the last one. Tempted to start an arbitrary conversation about the secret lives of dust mites or anything other than the things they were talking about, she didn't. That would be like running from the football player.

She really needed to do better. So, she put her hands on her hips and asked, "Any ideas?"

"Well, if awkward wins and boring loses, I think we just need to look bored."

That sounded simple. But her eyes kind of dropped to his lips, and an odd tingling sensation crept up her spine. She'd almost have termed it excitement, except that couldn't be right.

Her next guess would have been anticipation.

Maybe her confusion over her emotions caused the next words to tumble out. "Maybe we should practice."

Their eyes widened at the same time they met.

Immediately, she started shaking her head. "Never mind. That was a really stupid idea."

"No." His voice sounded strangled. "You're probably right. It probably would be a good idea to practice." His words were serious and slow, seeming to come out of his mouth without thought from him as he stared at her while invisible electrical charges swamped the air around them.

Uncomfortable yet exciting at the same time.

Which probably explained the odd urge she had to back up and move closer. Neither one made any sense.

But neither of them made any move to back their idea with action. It felt like several long years later that she practically tore her eyes away from his, shoved her hands in her pockets, and stared at the floor while she said, "It's late. I probably better get home."

Her words seemed to bring them out of their trance, and he moved, clearing his throat. "Yeah. Tomorrow is a big day."

She nodded, but it was still another minute before she finally slapped her leg and reached for the barn door.

"Let me," Martin said, moving at the same time she did. Their hands, both reaching for the wooden handle on the barn door, bumped into each other.

The ripples of excitement that had been going over her backbone shot up her arm from the contact.

Maybe he felt the same, because he seemed to shake his arm a little, but neither of them stopped reaching for the door handle, and their hands ended up landing side by side on it.

Both of them stood there, staring at their hands.

Blakely wanted to keep lying to herself. To tell herself that whatever those tingles of excitement and buzzing electrical current that seemed to flow between them was, it was just a passing thing and certainly didn't indicate changing feelings for her best friend.

But she knew the truth. And that was all wrong. But the thing that was starting to dawn inside of her, maybe it was hope, maybe it was wishful thinking, but as well as she knew Martin, she figured it was probably based in knowledge and reality, was that it wasn't just her who felt those strange new things.

It was Martin too.

And that made him all the more dangerous.

"I can get it." She ignored the feelings, the tingles, and everything else and stepped toward the door, sliding it open, taking her hand away, and striding out.

"Blakely."

She froze. A step away from the door but still standing in the patch of light that fell from the opening. Both of them knew her actions weren't normal, and neither were his. Normally, they'd be joking and laughing with each other as they walked out, hitting the lights and shrouding the barnyard in darkness broken only by snatches of moonlight and the glow of a million stars.

"Yeah?" Her word somehow sounded hopeful. She didn't know why.

"Careful driving home."
It was only a few short miles.
"I will."
"See you tomorrow."
"You too."

Chapter Fifteen

The festival didn't start until eleven.

Blakely was at his ranch early the next morning, helping him feed and also helping him move his bred heifers from the lower pasture where they'd pretty much grazed it down to the back sixty-acre piece.

If things were awkward between them last night, they'd gotten better this morning. She acted normal, and he supposed he did too, although he wasn't used to dealing with the ride of emotions that had been stirred in his chest.

Guilt being the primary one, because yesterday sometime, he couldn't even remember when the thought popped into his head, he had thought of a trick so brilliant, so perfect, that he couldn't believe that he hadn't thought of it before.

But all through their conversation last night, where they were talking about the fallout from her being unselfish, and putting Erin first, then sharing what she knew even though she knew that by sharing it, she was only hurting herself, his guilt had built.

Guilt wasn't the only emotion he was feeling though, because he couldn't stop thinking that maybe he didn't want Blakely as his best friend anymore.

He was looking at her more like a girlfriend.

A potential wife.

He wanted to kiss her.

He'd never wanted to kiss his best friend before in his life.

But the idea of practicing, the idea of being in the kissing contest today, he couldn't say he wasn't looking forward to it, because he was.

He'd actually dreamed about it during the night. An odd dream that had him riding broncs again and Blakely trick riding and them kissing from the backs of their horses and somehow kissing made the animals disappear and it was just Blakely and him, and neither of them missed what they didn't have anymore because they had each other.

Four romance novels was definitely too many for a man to read.

Although the dream wasn't entirely wrong. He'd been far more focused on Blakely and hadn't even thought about the rodeo circuit.

"They should be happy there for a while," Blakely said, shutting the gate and latching it.

He pushed his guilt aside. If God wanted her to win the competition and go with the traveling show, it didn't matter whether or not he told her about the trick.

If you could help your friend, and you don't, what does that say about your character?

God doesn't need me to help. If she's meant to win, she will.

His thoughts were true, both of them. Even though they seemed contradictory.

If Blakely could act right, even though she didn't feel like it, he ought to be able to too, even if he didn't want to.

He figured the only difference was that she wanted to feel right, and he didn't. He wanted to *be* right. And not be forced to do something he didn't want to, just because it was the right thing to do.

"They should. There's lots of grass in there, and it's knee-high. I expect them to be content in there for at least two weeks."

"In the meantime, if you're going to move them into the back corner piece next, we should probably work on fixing that fence sometime in the next two weeks."

"The corner piece hasn't been touched yet this spring, and I'd like to get them in it. But you're going to be pretty busy. With the competition and, before that, the festival."

Blakely's face twisted for a minute, almost as though his words hurt.

He froze with his mouth open as she climbed on her four-wheeler. Of course. She was probably thinking something about the competition, something about not winning it, being here and not out with the trick riding show.

He almost said something. Really, he did. But he couldn't quite get himself to be that selfless. He didn't want her to go, although he wanted the very best for her, and he wanted to see her succeed, and he would support that, but he couldn't be a party to helping her do something that would take her away for up to three years.

It was selfish, but he just couldn't get himself to do it.

She paused just before she started her machine and looked over at him. "Is that all you were gonna do today?"

"Yeah. Everything else can wait until after the festival. Thanks a lot for helping me."

She lifted her shoulder. "Of course."

She started her four-wheeler and motored away. He followed her slowly. Thinking.

He helped her load Candy and Kisses onto the trailer when they got back to the barn.

"I can handle mucking their stalls and getting them ready for tonight. You can go on in to the festival if you like. I know you want to brush them and get your tack ready, and I'm sure your mom has a million things she needs to do." They grinned, the easy friendship between them still there, but there was something else between them now, too. Maybe several things. "I'll be in in a bit."

"I'll wait on you, and we'll get breakfast together." Her statement was a question; she lifted her brow, waiting for his okay.

"Sounds good."

His guilt hadn't dissipated any by the time he finished morning chores and drove into town, parking at the festival lot.

He should have gone straight to the stable, where he knew Blakely most likely would be, unless her mother had gotten her busy with something else already. But he didn't.

He felt restless, along with the guilt. At the same time, there was this attraction that he knew he needed to fight.

For the first time, it made him drag his feet to go see her.

He welcomed the distraction when Whit Lewis pulled in with his cattle trailer and needed help unloading.

Martin stood with his foot on the bottom rail after the cattle were unloaded, watching as Whit and his boys—who were probably not more than eight or ten years old—maneuvered the cattle to the end stalls where they wanted them.

The boys were young, but anyone could see their pride in helping their dad and their love for what they were doing. Whit was also depending on his kids, and they worked together as a team.

Kind of the way he and his brothers had done growing up. He never really thought about it before, but he supposed he wanted a couple boys just like that for himself one day.

He supposed he always had, just hadn't been something he noticed. Maybe it was because he never really thought about any girl he'd want to settle down with, but those were the feelings he got when he looked at Blakely. The settling down kind of feelings.

While she was definitely not feeling anything of the kind. Rather, she was feeling the let-me-go-tour-the-country-with-the-traveling-western-show kind of feelings.

Pretty much the opposite of what he was feeling.

Not that he even gave a flip about his feelings. He never had.

Just these were a lot stronger and a lot harder to brush away.

"I figured I'd find you here," Pastor Race said as he propped a foot on the bottom rail, leaning his forearms on the top, settling into the spot next to Martin. "Usually, you and Blakely are inseparable. She here?"

"Yeah. She's somewhere around. I just haven't found her yet."

"Didn't look like you're looking too hard."

"I guess I'm kind of avoiding her."

Race shifted. "Really? I've never known you two to fight."

"We're not." Martin steepled his hands together, no longer looking at Whit and his boys, or the cattle, or anything that had to do with the festival. "I guess I just feel like things are shifting a little between us, and I'm not sure what to do about it."

That wasn't the entire truth, but he wasn't going to go around chatting with another man about this attraction that he was feeling for his best friend. Even if that man was his pastor and her father.

"Because she wants to leave?" Race asked, adjusting his stance so he was square with the fence, staring at his hands as well. His words sounded casual. Almost too casual, although Martin didn't pick up on that right away. "Or something else? Are you guys regretting shifting things around with the kissing contest and the rodeo?"

"I don't think so. Although that's probably what instigated everything."

That was just flat-out honesty. If he hadn't been thinking about kissing Blakely, he might not be struggling with these feelings. Although, maybe he would anyway. He tried to think back, because he was pretty sure he'd been attracted to Blakely for a while. But he just hadn't noticed or given any credence to those feelings.

"Everything?" Race prompted.

He couldn't tell Race about the attraction. Not that he was ashamed, and not that he thought Race wouldn't approve of him necessarily as a suitor for his daughter, but because he wasn't even sure what it meant, what it was he felt.

Before he could think too hard about it, because he figured Race probably wouldn't tell him what he wanted to hear, he said, "You know how Blakely is. She's always giving stuff away. She's pretty selfless."

Looking back, it was pretty nice to be friends with someone who succeeded more than she failed trying to put other people first. He supposed he was the biggest beneficiary of that beyond her family.

"She is," Race said, his tone implying he was waiting for more.

"I don't know if you know that she taught Erin her best trick. The one that only she knows with the forward somersault."

"I know the one you mean."

Of course, he did. He was her father. He'd seen practically every competition she'd been in.

Race scratched his head. "That was really what gave her the advantage in any competition. That was pretty selfless of her to show it to her biggest competition."

"Exactly. And maybe that makes me feel guilty, because she was selfless while I wasn't."

"What do you mean?" Maybe there was a touch of irritation in Race's voice, or maybe it was his imagination, because when he looked over, Race looked confused but not angry. There was always warmth and love on his face, and right now was no different.

"I mean, she taught Erin that trick even though she knew that if she did, and Erin performed that trick well, she'd be winning the competition and grabbing the spot that Blakely wanted. And yet, even though I've watched her do that and admired that type of self-sacrifice, I know I have an idea that could possibly give Blakely an edge, and yet, I've kept it to myself and haven't said a word to her."

"Because you don't want her to win?"

Martin let out a deep breath, shook his head, the war in his chest twisting his face. "I want her to win. I want her to do well. I want every good thing for her. Truly I do. Except, you're right, I don't want her to leave. And I suppose that has something to do with the way I feel about her changing and me being selfish, doing what's best for me instead of her."

"You don't like her? You don't want to be friends with her anymore?" Those were questions, but Race seemed to already know the answers as he asked them.

"The opposite." He took his hands down from the top rail and dropped his foot, turning toward Race. "Actually, I think I might be falling in love with her."

He hated the words as they were coming out of his mouth. Not because he didn't want to fall in love with Blakely, necessarily, but he didn't want to admit it. Had determined not to admit it. This wasn't exactly guy talk.

But he had never felt this mixed up and confused and torn before.

Funny, but Race didn't look the slightest bit surprised.

But the man didn't say *I figured*, or *I told you so*, or *that's what I thought.*

Instead, he straightened from leaning on the fence, dropping his foot and turning. "I guess that tells you what you need to do then, doesn't it?"

"What you mean?"

"If you think you're falling in love with her. I suppose the kind of 'love' most people think about is more the tingly feelings and the wanting to touch her and be with her. But true love, the kind of love a man should have for his wife, the kind a man should have for the woman he loves, is selfless."

Immediately, the verse that he'd memorized years and years ago for his church youth camp came into his head. *Charity suffered long and is kind...* It ran through his head until he got to the part that had been nagging at him—*seeketh not her own.*

That's what Race was saying. If he loved Blakely, if he truly loved her, he wouldn't be out for himself. He'd be out for her.

"But I don't think that her going out and winning a spot in the show is the best thing for her. She'll be gone a year and a half, maybe three years. Surely, as her dad, you don't want that either?"

"Of course not. You never want to see someone you love leave.

Maybe as her dad, I would give her suggestions as to what's best for her, and she might or might not take them. But I can't give her suggestions based on what I want. And sometimes what I want gets mixed up with what I think is best for her. Probably the same for you." Race gave him an eye, considering. His words didn't sound judgmental but were spoken with a deep love.

"I get what you're saying, it's not up to me to decide whether or not it's best for her to go with the trick riding show."

"You don't have the right. You're not a parent, you're not her husband."

"I know. But I'm a friend. Her best friend."

"I think it's probably your job to support her, love her, and let God handle the rest. That's really pretty much my job too." He gave a little guilty grin. "I don't always do that. Sometimes, I feel like I need to meddle."

He might feel like he needed to meddle, but he would never withhold something that could help her. Martin was sure of it. Not like he'd been doing.

It wasn't hard to see, if he loved Blakely, he had to tell her about the trick. And then, he'd probably have to help her learn it. And then, he'd have to watch her win the competition and leave.

Because God had been clear: love didn't seek its own.

He supposed the disappointment, sadness, and loneliness that he felt at the idea of Blakely leaving was something that he would bear, if he loved Blakely.

Race looked at the cattle in the pen thoughtfully. "Love, the world's definition of love between a man and woman, seems to make us do really stupid things sometimes. It has a tendency to make us jealous, and mean, and say things to people that we would never say to a casual friend. It's almost the opposite of what biblical love is supposed to be."

Martin could see that easily. He never thought about it before, but Race was absolutely right. People who claimed to love each other sometimes weren't very nice to each other. Weren't helpful at all and seemed to expect the other person to treat them like a king or queen while they sat on their throne voicing royal demands.

He wasn't demanding anything, and he wasn't being mean to Blakely, but he wasn't treating her the way he would like to be treated, which was probably the basis for all the things about love and that verse. It really all boiled down to deciding what he would want, then doing that for Blakely.

If she knew a trick that would help him win a competition, he'd be really angry at her if she didn't share it with him.

"Thanks. I needed this today."

"Anytime, son." Race clamped a hand on his shoulder. "I think sometimes we get the idea that love is a natural thing. But like with most things in the Bible, pretty much to do it right, you have to go against everything you're naturally inclined to do."

"I guess I need to tell Blakely about the trick."

"Do you? I don't want to see her go any more than you do."

He furrowed his brows at Race, confused.

"It's your decision. I was just telling you, from a pastor's perspective, about love. From a dad's perspective, I want to do everything in my power to keep Blakely here."

Martin supposed as a dad, he had a little more right to try to do that than he did. Regardless, there was no confusion in his mind anymore. He knew what he had to do. Now, he just needed to go do it.

Chapter Sixteen

Blakely walked along beside Candy, the lead rope in her hand, leading her, while Darcy sat on her back, gripping her mane and looking slightly scared.

Blakely remembered vividly the first time she was on a horse. Neither one of her parents had been horse people, and she hadn't ever ridden before, but she begged for lessons until, when she was eight, her parents had gifted them to her for her birthday.

Best birthday gift ever.

She would be eternally grateful to Race and Penny for continuing those lessons after her parents died and she and her siblings came to their house.

The death of her parents had left a big, gaping hole in her heart, and the foster family she'd gone to before Race and Penny had adopted them had lived in town and had been all into sports. Basketball, football, volleyball, even hockey. They'd been good people, at least she thought of them that way from her little-girl perspective, but horseback riding hadn't even been on their radar, let alone trick riding.

They'd wanted her to forget about the horses and put on a uniform.

Thankfully, she hadn't been there long, and Race and Penny had seemed to know how important having horses in her life was. She liked to think she was over her parents' death, or at least mostly over. She wasn't sure a person ever got over losing their parents, no matter how old they were and no matter how they died. But the horses gave her something to focus on, something to care about, something that she felt she was good at, and they helped.

Maybe that's what had given her the idea of giving lessons to the foster kids her parents brought in, thinking it would be good for them, like it had been for her.

"Thanks so much for giving her a ride, Blakely," her mom said as she walked around the corner of the barn.

"Anytime. I think Candy likes her." She grinned up at Darcy, who, although she was sitting stiffly, with her hands clenched in Candy's mane, puffed out her chest just a little and smiled, only a bit tight around the edges.

"Do you really think so?"

"I do. Candy is a very good judge of people, and she likes little girls especially."

Darcy grinned and loosened her hand enough to move it up and down, tapping Candy's neck with her closed fist, because she couldn't quite get herself to let go of her death grip on the mane.

"Blakely will give you a riding lesson later this week. But for now, we need to go get the gingerbread men out and set up for the decorating contest. I know you said you wanted to help with that," Penny said, tilting her head at Darcy.

If it had been her, Blakely knew she wouldn't have wanted to go do anything else other than be with the horses, but Darcy wasn't quite as smitten, because she nodded, her little chin going up and down and her eyes lighting up at the thought of decorating gingerbread men.

Penny lifted her arms up, and Darcy leaned into them, only

letting go of the mane at the last minute when she was sure Miss Penny would catch her.

"Where's Frank?"

"He's with Dante. He hasn't wanted to be anywhere else, and Dante's been humoring him." Miss Penny lifted a brow at Blakely. "He really is a nice man."

Goodness, she had no idea how her mother did it, but somehow, she always found out about the stupid stuff that Blakely did.

"Did Journee tell you about me being in the loft?"

"It wasn't Journee."

"Oh?"

"No. Mrs. Walter happened to be walking by the end of the barn when, as she described it, your eyes landed on Dante, your face pretty much exploded into some kind of weird, twisted, chainsaw-murdering type shape, and then you tucked your tail between your legs," here, Penny lifted a brow, "which made me want to ask if there's something you needed to tell me..."

"No."

Penny's lips pursed before she continued. "And you went running for the hayloft ladder. Mrs. Walter, of course, thought your behavior quite odd and thought maybe I needed to know about it."

"This is what I get for being a PK."

"Being a preacher's kid has nothing to do with it. She was just a concerned lady of the church, letting me know that my almost thirty-year-old daughter was acting like a three-year-old." Penny had no heat behind her words, and they were laced with a good bit of sarcasm, and Blakely knew she wasn't truly in trouble, but...

"I'm sorry, Mom. You're right. Mrs. Walter had the story completely accurate, except for the tail."

"The detail of the tail almost made me doubt the whole story."

"The rest of it's right." She fingered the lead rope in her hand and smiled a little as Candy nuzzled her ear, pushing a bit with her muzzle, as a reminder to Blakely that she was still standing there.

"He's had Frank all morning." Her mother didn't need to say

anything more. She didn't even need to say that much. Just looking, not exactly disappointed, but a look that said she expected better behavior out of Blakely. Kindness. Maybe even maturity.

"I'm sorry, Mom. I felt like Dad was kinda pushing me toward him, because he asked me to go with him to the horse show. And…" She put a hand up around Candy's neck, pushing her cheek against the other side into her mane. There was just something about horses that had always comforted her. "I guess you know at the foster family that I stayed with, they were all about sports. And I wasn't there long, but it was enough. I mean…"

"I understand. It's okay. There are bad things about everything. I get that you could have watched athletes and seen sometimes they come off as arrogant. Sometimes, all the adulation that they have goes to their head. There are bad apples. Men who are egocentric. Even ladies who start to believe all the good things that are told about them and forget that they have fears and failures just like everyone else."

"I know. I know that in order to be an elite athlete and play on the level that Dante plays on, it takes a lot of sacrifice and a lot of work and a lot of effort, and you really are something that other people aren't. Or you have something that other people don't. But… I guess I just had that shoved down my throat, and in order to do that, they took my horses away from me. Which I know is stupid, but maybe for a girl who'd just lost her parents…"

Penny let go of Darcy's hand and closed the distance between Blakely and her, wrapping her arms around Blakely, who leaned away from her horse and into her mother. "I wasn't giving you a hard time about it. I have hang-ups, and you don't throw them in my face every time I see you. I don't want to do that to you either. And I feel just now, from what you said, that I did. I'm sorry. If you want to hate athletes for the rest of your life, and if you want to hate football players, and if you want to run away from them, that's fine. I'm going to love you anyway. And I'm going to look at myself and work on my own issues and failures. Because there's a lot there to work on."

"You know what, Mom? There's not. Sometimes, I think you and Dad are perfect. And here you say that you have issues and failures just like everyone else, and it makes me kind of think that I don't know you very well. Because I don't see them."

"They're there. Maybe sometimes, it's the issues in our head. The things we fight but no one else can see, and maybe our actions are right, but we just don't quite have our heart there yet."

It was like her mom had been sitting in her brain for the last week. "You struggle with that too?"

"I sure do. You know, it's almost easy to do right when your heart's right, isn't it? It's doing right when you don't want to that's really hard."

"It's like you've been in my pocket since I lost the competition. That has been my struggle. There are things I know I need to do, to be nice and kind, but..." She thought of Erin and the trick that she'd shown her. "You're right. Sometimes, I can make myself do things that I know no one's supposed to do, but it's like my heart is sitting there in my chest with its arms crossed, tapping its foot and pouting because it's not getting its way."

"I think that's life. Making ourselves do things we don't want to do just because we know they're right." Her mom leaned back, both hands on her upper arms, and looked directly into Blakely's eyes. "Your dad might have been nudging you toward Dante a little, but I think there's someone else who's better for you. And I think your dad knows that too. Maybe, your dad had ulterior motives?"

Blakely's brows knotted together. "What do you mean?"

She couldn't imagine her dad doing anything underhanded.

Her mom lifted her shoulder and kind of gave a "what am I going to do about it" look. "Your dad just knows how you are. And when you get pushed, you push back, often going in a different direction." Her mom's lips turned up slowly. "It's funny, because you train that out of your horses."

Blakely just blinked at her mom, her eyelids going up and down. It was a truth she'd never heard before. And it was so true. She couldn't believe she hadn't seen it in herself. Funny how one can be blind to one's own flaws.

"If you're okay, I'm good to grab Darcy and go get these gingerbread guys set up."

"Thanks, Mom. I needed what you had to say."

"I needed our chat too. I think sometimes I expect my children to be perfect. And that's hardly fair when I'm so far from it myself."

For some reason, that statement made Blakely's eyes fill up with tears. She blinked them back. She wanted to be perfect. Not necessarily for any great award or to make herself look good, just because her parents had done so much for her, more than she could ever repay, and she wanted them to be proud of her.

Her mom lifted a hand and wiggled her fingers.

Blakely kissed her fingers and waved back, her heart full. She felt like God had done a horrible thing to her when he'd taken her parents. Then, when she ended up in a foster home that hadn't been interested in horses but had tried to force her to be an athlete, she'd resented that too. Maybe that was where she started to push back when she felt pushed into something.

That was definitely where her distaste or, more likely, distrust of athletes had happened as well.

It was high time she overcame those flaws.

But her mom had said something else of interest.

Someone else who's better for you.

Blakely grunted. She could almost tell who her mom had been thinking of. Her mom knew her better than she knew herself.

She was almost sure that her mom had been thinking of Martin.

Maybe all of her struggle with giving up the secret to her trick and helping Erin, almost ensuring that Erin would win the place in the show, wasn't about Blakely not fulfilling her dream and was about God having a different plan, one she hadn't seen but one that she thought she might be glimpsing.

One she thought she really might like.

She thought, after the conversation with her mom, knowing that her mom and maybe even her dad thought Martin was perfect for her had helped her awaken to the attraction herself, and then shifting that in with the idea that she was actually helping her competition beat her...

She almost laughed. Could it really be what the Lord was thinking? That she was actually helping herself by helping her competition?

After all, she'd be gone for a year and a half.

Or three years.

She'd be thirty. Martin would be too. He could be married by the time she got back.

Is that what she wanted?

To be thirty years old and just arriving back home to figure out what she would do with the rest of her life? To see her best friend married to someone else?

Candy shook her head, bobbing it up and down, and Blakely snapped out of her thoughts to see Frank and Dante approaching.

Oh boy. She hadn't even had time to think about what she was going to say. But she figured it had better include an apology.

Funny, because the temptation to run was still there, but she dug her heels in. After all, if she had a tendency to be contrary, she should put it to good use. If her heart wanted her to run backward, she'd force herself to walk forward.

Chapter Seventeen

Blakely didn't even wait for them to get to her. She walked to them and started talking before she even reached them.

"I'm sorry about yesterday. Maybe you didn't notice, maybe you heard about it, but when I saw you, I ran. And that was really rude. And I'm sorry."

She felt like she should say a lot more. Explain why or at least explain about her aversion to athletes, or about her parents pushing her into him, or about something. But they were not really explanations more than they were excuses. She wasn't going to use them as a crutch.

"Actually, I did notice. I saw your boots, and I also saw you in the hayloft. I wasn't entirely sure that you're running from me, but I suspected."

He shifted, the way athletes often did, like their muscles were uncomfortably large and they were readjusting them. "It was actually kind of refreshing. Most of the time, I have the problem of people rushing toward me. Wanting something. An autograph, to talk to me, time, or just, I don't know, something from me. It was pretty nice, actually, to not get bulldozed over by adoring fans. But to have someone run from me. Yeah, it was a little hard on my ego, but I liked it."

Blakely shook her head. "That's awfully nice of you to try to make me feel better, but I know I shouldn't have done it. I'm sorry."

"You better take that to the bank. Blakely apologizing doesn't happen very often." Martin came over, and Blakely's stomach practically jumped out of her chest when he put his arm around her and pulled her toward him.

She went, and she thought she kept the surprise off her face, but it felt weird. Weird but good. He was warm and solid beside her, and she liked that.

"I guess I should have recorded it?" Dante asked with a wink.

"Definitely. I think there are people who would pay to see that." Martin's voice held humor.

Tempted to jab him in the ribs, a gesture that this new position of being squeezed up beside him allowed, Blakely refrained.

"Well, I'd promised Frank that he and I would throw the football together some before I go back and let Journee paint my face."

"Oh. Ouch. Sounds like someone lost a bet."

"Something like that." One side of Dante's mouth hitched up in a grin, and Blakely could admit that maybe he wasn't troll ugly.

Dante sauntered off, Frank holding tight to one of the large hands, and suddenly, her position snuggled into Martin felt a little weird.

Or maybe that was just her immaturity poking its head up again.

"What's the matter?"

"How do you know there's anything wrong?" She looked up at him, and he looked down with an affectionate grin. One she hadn't seen too much of. She liked it.

"I felt you tense. You're worried about the kissing contest?" He grabbed his phone out of his pocket and checked the time. "We've got an hour."

"Why did they have to start the festival off with that?"

"I guess they must want to get people here on time. I've heard it's pretty popular." He raised a brow at her. "You're not answering my question."

"Yeah. I guess it's the kissing contest."

"Maybe we should have practiced after all." His words sounded casual, but she felt like they were laced with something a little deeper.

"It's too late now." She fingered the lead rope in her hand, Candy waiting patiently behind her.

"Yeah. I guess we'll just have to wing it. I think we can do it. You and I have made a pretty good team over the years."

Again, she felt like there was something more in his tone. Or maybe it was just that she wanted there to be.

"Hey, lady."

Blakely looked down to see two little girls in pigtails, one a little older than the other, maybe six and eight, staring up at her with identical big brown eyes.

"Will you give us a ride on your horse?"

"I sure will." She smoothed down the red ribbons that she'd braided into Candy's hair. "Did your parents say it was okay?" Blakely looked around and then saw Mrs. Walter from church standing a little ways away.

"Those are my grandchildren, Ariel and Paige. I told them they might be able to talk you into giving them a ride before the festival starts."

"That they did." Blakely smiled affectionately at the cute little girls.

"I'll lift one up and stand back and wait with the other one. Who's going first?" Martin moved around, dropping his arm from her and shifting away.

Despite the heat of the summer morning, she missed his warmth beside her. Maybe that was what it was like to stand shoulder to shoulder with someone. She doubted it though. It probably made a difference if she loved the person she was standing with.

Did she love Martin?

Definitely. As a friend.

She had a feeling it went deeper. But she didn't examine it too much while she gave the girls rides, not taking too long, because she needed to get Candy put away and make it to the kissing contest. Although, missing it wouldn't upset her either.

There were more people milling about, commenting on the wreaths that were hanging on all the stall doors and the Christmas lights that blinked merrily along the inside of the barn as they wandered down through.

Martin stood in the stall with Candy while Blakely brushed her down.

"I have something that I want to talk to you about."

"Okay?" she said.

He'd been kinda quiet the whole time they'd been giving rides. Usually, he was funny and quite entertaining and charming even. It made sense that there was something on his mind.

"I guess there's no other way to do it than to come right out and say it," he said, without saying whatever it was he wanted to say.

Which made her smile. "Like you just did?"

He laughed, pushing her on the shoulder playfully. "If you're going to make fun of me, I'm not going to talk to you."

"Oh, that's real mature. And here I thought I was the one with maturity problems."

"You are. I just happen to imitate you sometimes."

"Right. And so far, you've not said anything that I don't already know. Was there something new you want to talk about?"

"Actually, yes."

She ran the brush one last time down Candy's back, then dropped her hand and raised her eyes. "I'm listening."

"I thought of a trick for you. One I think will be pretty easy to learn. And one, if you can do it, I've never seen anyone else do, and I think will help you win the competition." His eyes were steady on hers, although it felt like something flickered, maybe just a small tremor through his body. "If that's what you want."

"Of course, that's what I want! It's what I've worked for for years. You know that." Maybe her voice was a little more incredulous than it might have been otherwise, because she actually had been thinking that maybe that wasn't what she wanted. It felt weird now that not only was her mom underlining the feelings that she'd been having for her best friend, but now Martin himself was questioning whether this was actually what she wanted.

And this was what she was talking about. Her contrariness.

She dropped her head right away. Was it? Was this her feeling that people were pushing her in one direction, so she balked and went in a different one?

Immediately, she knew it to be true. Her mom was right. She trained that out of her horse. She needed to train that out of herself.

Still, it wouldn't hurt to find out.

"Do your trick backward," Martin said simply, shortly, and... brilliantly.

She knew she probably looked ridiculous as she stared off into space, her mouth half open, her eyes wide but not seeing anything as she ran through the trick in her head. The galloping of the horse, riding backward, having her stop, staying loose, flying out of the saddle, and, yeah, a backward flip, which would land her facing the back of the horse, but still, brilliant.

"I cannot believe I did not think of that myself." She shook her head. "That is the most ingenious thing ever. Of course. Backward." Excitement bubbled up inside of her, and gratitude was right there with it, filling her chest and overflowing, making her eyes shine, and making it hard to stand still. "Thank you. That is so fantastic. Of course. And unveiling it at the finals? Absolutely astounding. We will blow them away. Man, I knew there was a reason you're my best friend."

She was excited, but she wasn't too excited to see that while

Martin was happy for her, there was a shadow of something over his face that kept him from looking completely and totally ecstatic.

What was it?

Chapter Eighteen

utterflies swirled in Blakely's stomach as they walked into the large community center building for the kissing contest.

She couldn't believe what Martin had thought of. She'd been over-the-moon excited.

Crazy, because she'd almost decided that God had actually not wanted her to win the competition, wanted her to stay home.

But what other sign did she need?

Martin coming up with the perfect trick for her to do, one that would give her the advantage over Erin too.

Erin had beauty and grace, which Blakely knew she was lacking, but she'd been the technical leader all along, and now with that playing field way back in her favor, she was pretty sure she could win.

If the kissing contest had been right then when Martin told her, they probably would have won that, too. At least if enthusiasm and excitement were voted on.

She definitely wanted to jump on him and wrap her arms around him and skip up and down and scream and yell.

She'd actually been kind of proud of her decorum.

But they'd made the long walk to the community building, her nervousness growing. Martin held the door for her, and she walked in. Somehow, snow swirled out of the air vents.

Not real snow but tiny pieces of something white and sparkling.

"They must really have the air turned down low. It's cold in here," Martin said from behind her as the door clicked shut.

"And it's packed," she whispered as he came up alongside her.

Several people greeted them as they walked slowly toward the front.

"It looks to me like they might have changed the way they do things. It kind of looks like..." Martin's voice trailed off.

"They said that judges judge, but that sign at the front by the table is saying pick your winner."

"I guess they'll tell us. But I don't like being surprised at the last minute."

Blakely didn't either. This was going to be hard enough without having weird rule changes. "Journee said the judges were supposed to watch the kiss and choose a winner." She crossed her arms over her chest, feeling like the rug had been yanked out from underneath her. "Looks like there are buckets or something in front of the seats."

"Hey, I'm not sure what that's all about. They say 'vote here' on them."

Several other couples were already milling about at the front, and Blakely and Martin greeted them as they got closer.

"Great. Our last couple is here." Mrs. Hutchison, the lady in charge of the kissing contest every year since its instigation, walked over.

Curvy and trim, Mrs. Hutchinson was probably in her forties but didn't look nearly that old, and she didn't exactly ooze sex appeal, but she definitely had a flirty smile always hovering on the corners of her lips.

Ten years ago, her husband had been killed in a military training accident, leaving her alone with two small children to raise.

She hadn't remarried, and her kids were now teens.

Blakely always liked her, just because she seemed like so much fun to be around.

But she'd never participated in the kissing contest. Maybe it would change her opinion of Mrs. Hutchison. Not because of Mrs. Hutchison, but because of the negative aspects she'd be associating with the contest. Except...she slanted a glance at Martin. An odd shiver shimmied across her chest.

Maybe not.

"Okay, gather around, folks. We changed the rules a bit this year, I'm sure you've noticed, and I want to explain things to you. Then, I'm gonna explain them to the audience. So you'll get them a second time. But I'll answer any questions before I do."

Mrs. Hutchison looked down at her clipboard and then up at each couple, checking names off. Apparently making sure everyone was there.

"All right, this year, we've made the kissing contest into a charity event. All proceeds that we raise from this will go toward the Secret Santa ministry the church has. No one gets paid for that, but the money will go to buy gifts, groceries, and the other things the Secret Santas give out. I'm sure all of you have heard about the good that the program does in church."

Blakely looked at the sign that hung on the back wall, not really reading it, just trying to look at anything that would distract her from the riot in her chest and the man beside her and the crowd of people waiting and what she was going to have to do in just a few short minutes.

The Christmas tree blinked in the corner, and suddenly, she took a keen interest in the decorations.

She could do this. Part of her wanted to do this. And part of her wanted to run. She just hoped it wasn't the bigger part.

Chapter Nineteen

Martin listened to Mrs. Hutchison with half an ear, his stomach pulling in tight. Painfully.

It wasn't that he didn't want to kiss Blakely. And it wasn't that he was nervous about kissing her.

He'd come to the conclusion, that's what he wanted.

The problem was he didn't really want it like this.

Not as a competition, in front of hundreds of people, trying to make it into a show.

Maybe, if they were like Heavenne and Aiden, the couple who was just out of high school, and had been together for a year or two, it might be different.

Or Connie Brockett and Larry Zigler, the retired couple, Both of them were widowed, having lost their spouses, and they were having a second chance romance.

In fact, all of the couples were couples who had been together, dating, at least for months, if not years.

He couldn't figure out why Race would have asked him to be in the contest with Krissy, when they weren't even a couple.

Something nagged him. Something that he thought he was missing. Something that he felt he should know.

"Okay everyone. Take your places behind your buckets. Each couple will have their chance in the spotlight. So be ready. After everyone has had an opportunity to show the crowd your kiss, people will come up and vote on it by putting money in your bucket. The person with the most money in their bucket wins."

Mrs. Hutchison smiled, her eyes crinkling, and looking for all the world that she was getting ready to enjoy the next however long it took.

Martin figured he probably looked like he was going to throw up.

Blakely was uncharacteristically quiet and still.

Normally she dove into everything as hard as she could and didn't stand in the background.

But she wasn't cracking jokes, and she wasn't out in the front.

He put an arm around her and leaned down. "Are you okay?"

She nodded. It wasn't very convincing to him.

She should have looked up at him with laughing eyes and made some kind of wisecrack about him being afraid and her needing to comfort him or something.

The fact that she didn't told him all he needed to know about how she felt about this.

Blakely was scared.

They walked over to their bucket and settled down in the two chairs behind it. There hadn't been too much talking among the contestants, and there was none now as Mrs. Hutchison stood in front of the packed building and explained the rules to everyone sitting there. The Christmas music that had been playing in the background was turned down low as she spoke, and the crowd was quiet.

As Martin looked over the faces, they seem to be pleased with this new turn of events, and the way the contest had changed. It seemed like the people were pretty excited that they got to choose the winner, that *they* were the judges.

His eyes scanned the crowd, finally settling on Pastor Race, standing in the back leaning against the wall, his arms crossed over his chest.

There seem to be a little smile on his face.

It was that smile that made Martin's eyes pause, his head churn with thoughts, and his brow wrinkle.

The man almost looked smug.

And that was when that elusive something gelled inside his head.

Blakely and her contrary streak.

She always pushed back when she felt she was being pushed.

But, she fought harder if she felt what she wanted was slipping out of her grasp.

Was it possible that Pastor Race was up to his matchmaking with Blakely, only instead of wanting Blakely to be with Dante, he actually wanted Blakely to be with Martin?

That seemed kind of far-fetched; a little bit too complicated for his simple brain. Simple when it came to romance, anyway.

Not that he wasn't able to figure complicated things out, he just didn't typically sit around thinking about romance and the different aspects of it...there were far too many feelings involved for him to be able to figure that accurately.

But, this was the first time that he'd realized that he'd fallen in love with his best friend.

He supposed new thought patterns were inevitable.

Mrs. Huchison started down at the opposite end of the table thankfully. I'm dreaming of a white Christmas played softly while she introduced Connie and Larry and all eyes turned to them.

All eyes except Martin's. He didn't watch. Because he knew what he was going to do. He'd decided what kind of kiss he was going to give Blakely.

She probably had plans about the kind of kiss she was going to give him. He almost grinned at the thought.

Regardless, he knew what he was going to do. What he needed to do, to be fair to Blakely.

The crowd roared with approval, and Blakely shifted beside him.

He glanced over. she was biting her lip.

"If this were a trick riding competition, you'd be pacing and slapping a rope or gloves or something against your leg, as you strode back and forth. It's probably hard for you to sit and wait."

Her smile was pinched, but it was there. And her eyes crinkled a little. "We've been through that a lot haven't we?"

He nodded.

"If this were a rodeo, you'd be leaning against the fence, one foot on the bottom rung, forearms balanced over the top, and you'd be staring off into space. Not talking to anyone, and probably running through the typical pattern of whatever bronc you drew."

Her eyes were knowing, and he had to agree she was dead on.

The smiles they shared were small but real. They knew each other.

"So this is just a little different. We've both been through this kind of thing before, just never had to sit in front of a bunch people get stared at what we..."

"Have to say, I'm a lot more comfortable trick riding in front of people than I am kissing."

He didn't miss the little quiver in her voice, even though her face looked brave, her chin up.

"Does your stomach feel like you swallowed a bunch of steel wool?"

Her smile grew wider. "Are you admitting to being nervous?"

"Sure as shooting."

Her breath puffed out, and she said, "Not only did I swallow it, someone's inside and they're using it."

A roar went up from the crowd again, and Martin realized he hadn't even been paying attention. Not when Mrs. Hutchison was talking between contestants, and not even to know how many people had gone.

The couple beside them hadn't gone, so they still had a little bit of time.

Blakely picked at her fingernail, and he took her hand in his, holding it still. She gave him a grateful smile.

About three seconds went by before she leaned over and whispered, "Do normal towns do this kind of thing?"

"Is it just now occurring to you to question it?"

"I should have questioned it a long time ago shouldn't I?" She grunted. "About the time you asked me to do this with you."

"I think you volunteered."

"I probably did. I'm dumb like that sometimes."

"Come on. Can't be that bad. Seriously, is kissing me worse than potentially falling off a horse? And every time you go out in a trick riding competition, every time you even practice, you're taking a chance. Really, you've kinda hurt my feelings."

"I'm sorry, but yes. Yes it is. It is much worse than falling off a horse. I would rather fall off a horse one hundred times than have to sit in front of all these people and have them watch me kiss someone."

"It's not just someone. It's me." He tried to say it lightly, but her words had scraped his heart.

He wasn't exactly jumping up and down in anticipation at the thought of kissing in front of all these people, but the idea of kissing Blakely had been growing on him, until, he definitely wanted to.

But he couldn't hardly admit that to her.

Not now.

He needed to be careful, or she might figure it out.

More cheers, and Martin lifted his head, to see Hannah and Brendan beside them, kissing.

And kissing.

And kissing.

Catcalls from the audience, and louder cheers, and some people were even stamping their feet. Basically the entire building was a rumbling noise.

Blakely had glanced over, and she looked back at him, her eyes wide and more scared than he'd ever seen them in her life before, and that was saying something considering how much time they'd spent together, and how many things they'd done where he actually expected her to be petrified.

Her hand twisted in his, and their fingers threaded together. She squeezed, her knuckles white.

"It's okay," he said. Nervous himself, but for slightly different reasons.

"Don't think we have to worry about losing. I think that's going to be a pretty hard thing to beat," she said with another side glance at Hannah and Brendan who were still kissing.

"I think Mrs. Hutchison's about ready to interrupt them."

"You think they could get disqualified for kissing too long?"

"She probably told us before we started, but I wasn't really paying attention."

"Me either. I'm assuming that is definitely not going to apply to us." Even as she said it, her eyes went to his, and she sounded hopeful rather than confident.

"I'm with you on that."

"We really should have talked about this more."

"I think we should have practiced." He lifted his shoulder, casually. "You never go to trick riding competitions and I certainly wouldn't ride a bronc without practicing. This shouldn't be any different."

"I'm in total agreement. Why did we not practice?"

"I think is too late," he murmured as Mrs. Hutchison stood in front of Hannah and Brandon and clapped her hands.

They broke apart. Yells and cheers filled the auditorium again.

Brennan jumped out of his chair and shouted to the audience, "I just want to announce that Hannah has agreed to marry me." He shot a fist in the air. Hannah stood up beside him, and they began kissing again.

"Yeah. Not going to compete with that," Martin murmured.

Their eyes met.

Martin looked at Blakely, truly looked at her, for the first time since he sat down. He thought, he could be wrong, but he thought that her nervousness and the fear that radiated from her wasn't about the kiss.

Her hand, strong and capable, the one that had worked beside him for years and now lay entwined with his, twitched.

Maybe she'd seen the same thing in his eyes. Something more than just a kissing contest.

"And now we have Blakely Barclay and Martin Zedler."

Mrs. Hutchison had finally gotten Hannah and Brennan separated. They sat back down, Hannah glowed. Brennan looked pretty proud of himself.

And funny, because Martin felt envious.

It clarified for him immediately why he wasn't more broken up about leaving the rodeo circuit.

That wasn't where his heart was anymore.

Probably, he'd known that from the first.

Maybe it was because of Blakely planning to audition for the trick show, that had made him realize that he didn't want her gone for a year and half. And he didn't want to be away from her.

It had been a slow realization, but with that look on Brennan's face, everything had become crystal clear to him now. He wanted that look.

Because he'd fallen in love with his best friend, and now he didn't know what to do about it.

"Go ahead you two. Your turn," Mrs. Hutchison prodded.

Everything that he'd just realized stumbled around in his head, and the words wanted to come out of his mouth. To tell her. Hoping that he wasn't wrong about what he'd seen on her face, and in her eyes, but this wasn't the time.

It also wasn't the time for a first kiss.

Mrs. Hutchison had moved off to the side, and Martin turned toward Blakely.

He let go of her hand and used both of his to cup her cheeks. Looking into her eyes.

The hall was completely quiet except for the dulcet tones of *I'll be home for Christmas* which piped out of the speakers. Even that seemed muted. Especially after all of the crazy noise from Brennan and Hannah's kiss.

Martin swallowed. He hoped he wasn't making a mistake. If only there'd been time to talk to Blakely about his plan.

Blakely looked into his eyes, trusting. Of course she was trusting. He trusted her just as much. They'd worked so much together, done so much, they'd always looked out for each other.

He hoped she understood that's what he was doing now.

Her skin was soft under his palms, her bones far more delicate than he would have expected if he'd even thought of it.

He couldn't keep from running his thumb over her cheekbone, and he couldn't quite get his breathing under control. It sounded harsh in the soft stillness of the room.

The rest of the world faded, and all he saw was Blakely. Felt her breath on his wrists and saw everything he'd ever wanted in her eyes.

Leaning in, he stretched toward her, and she closed her eyes.

His eyes closed too; he almost squeezed them shut, and his breath trembled. He moved just that much closer and placed his lips on her forehead.

Her scent, fresh with a touch of sweetness and a touch of wildness and so familiar surrounded him.

His hands trembled, and his heart shook. He didn't want to lift his head, lean back, move away, to let go.

He wanted more, had known he would, but he hadn't wanted to be disrespectful, hadn't wanted to kiss her and have it mean nothing, hadn't wanted to do that to Blakely, and hadn't wanted to do that to *them*.

Because what he had with Blakely was more important than a kissing contest, and more important than his ego, and more important than what the town expected of them. He wasn't going to take a chance of ruining that, not for the entertainment of the town or for the most important festival or the most important contest in the town of Mistletoe in the entire year. Not for anything.

Blakely meant too much to him for that.

He had expected catcalls, or boos, and a lot of ribbing and teasing, but, as he lifted his lips from her forehead and leaned back with what felt like his heart in his eyes, looking at Blakely the way a man looks at a woman when all he wants is to hear her laughter and see her smile and feel her touch and breathe her air and never leave her again, the way a man looks at the woman he loves and wants to spend the rest of his life with, the entire room full of hundreds of people was completely silent. Not even the Christmas music played.

"You didn't want to kiss me?" Blakely asked, hurt in her eyes. She blinked, and his heart constricted to think there might be tears there too.

He shook his head slightly, but right away. He didn't want her thinking that.

"I did. I do. But I didn't want to reduce us to competition. Not when I hadn't had a chance to tell you how I feel."

"How you feel?" Her words just barely audible, and her face wrinkled in confusion.

Probably because he never talked about how he felt.

She typically didn't either.

It just wasn't part of who they were, but if everything that he wanted had a chance of being reality, that needed to change.

His breath still trembled and he found it hard to fill his lungs. His words came out soft, meant only for her. "For a while now, I've been looking at you a little differently, feeling things that I've never felt before, and if I kissed you…I would mean it. Because I love you."

So many emotions went through her expressive eyes. Surprise, happiness, but the look that landed there last was a soft one, soft for his girl, because she was tough. And strong. And determined and stubborn and kind and sweet and generous and fearless and considerate and totally and completely selfless.

How could he not love her?

Wonder spread across her features. "It's happened to me too. I've fallen in love with my best friend."

He couldn't have stopped himself from smiling on the threat of his life. Nor did he want to.

"Now we could have that awkward first kiss?" she asked, her face glowing, a grin tugging both corners of her lips up.

"The one that is guaranteed to win us the contest?" he asked humor lacing his tone.

"Yeah. That one."

"Remember if we win, the folks in Mistletoe are gonna want you to be kissing me a lot."

"I like it when the townspeople and I agree on something."

They were both smiling as he lowered his head again, and she lifted hers to meet him. He tilted his just a little, at the same time she tilted hers the same way, and their noses bumped.

She giggled.

There were titters through the audience, as they both turned their head the other way, and their noses got in the way again.

"I don't think we could have been any more awkward if we'd have practiced it," he said, trying not to laugh.

"You need to quit smiling, or I think we'll have issues with our teeth as well."

"This is a kissing contest, no biting."

"I didn't say anything about biting, but you know, you have teeth in your mouth, I have teeth in my mouth, we gotta keep them from meeting in an awkward way."

"You're way over-thinking this, Whiplash. Just shut up and kiss me."

"Whatever you say, Staples."

This time when he lowered his head, he used the hands that were still cupping her cheek to tilt her head in the opposite direction of his, and their lips finally met.

He was in a bubble with Blakely, and had, quite honestly, forgotten about the crowd and the people in the contest as his hand slipped around her head, and she leaned closer to him gripping his shoulder, and making a sweet sound that he was pretty sure meant she was enjoying what they were doing.

Maybe he made a sound of his own, he couldn't say for sure.

All time seemed to stand still, and he was shocked and startled when Mrs. Hutchison tapped on both of their shoulders and said, "This is by far the sweetest kiss in all my years of running the kissing contest, and it also might be the longest. But you two need to stop."

He pulled back, shaky, and glad he was sitting down.

Blakely looked exactly the same way, and he couldn't say he minded the shakiness because the love shining in her eyes was more than enough for him.

Chapter Twenty

"You're going to do great," Martin said to Blakely as she paced back and forth.

"If I do, it's all because of you." She spoke without stopping, continuing to pace back and forth.

She couldn't be still, not before competition. There was just too much pent up energy in her.

Usually it worked out well. The horses could sense her energy, and that seemed to feed their own levels, and they all competed better.

She'd heard of horses that didn't, who could sense their rider's nervousness, and did worse during competitions. Thankfully, neither Candy nor Kisses were horses like that.

"I'll take some credit for that, but you're the one who worked on it, and caught on quickly."

"It's just like the frontwards one. Same key. I can't believe I didn't think of it."

"That's just God's way of saying you need me."

She stopped. Turning and facing him with only feet separating them. "I do." In the days since the kissing contest, the town, true to form had them kissing every day they met at the diner.

Not that either of them minded.

In fact, they didn't need anyone from the town asking them in order for them to just randomly stop on the sidewalk and practice.

But, as the competition drew nearer, and she nailed the backwards flip, Martin hadn't said anything, in fact, had indicated that he might spend whatever time he could spare from the ranch going to her shows across the country, Blakely had begun to realize that maybe what she thought she wanted all along wasn't what she really wanted.

Maybe God had been pushing her to give it up, because it wasn't His plan for her.

And, looking at Martin, she thought she was good with a new plan.

Except, this had been a dream. And her fingers, unimpressed by her feelings, were still clenched tight around it. She didn't want to give it up. Hadn't been able to get herself to do so. Not yet.

She couldn't stop herself from working as hard as she could for that last chance to do what she had dreamed of all her life. If she won, if she got the spot, she'd come back as soon as it was over, and beg Martin to marry her, if that's what she had to do.

She closed the distance between them, and put her arms around his shoulders, pressing herself against him. "Maybe there's something better I can do now rather than pacing before competition."

"Yeah? What would that be?" His hands ran up her back.

"I don't know. Let's think hard. Maybe we can figure something out."

"I think we're pretty good at spur of the moment improvising."

"I think you're right."

Kissing Martin was a lot better than pacing, and she made a mental note to remember that, as she led Candy and Kisses to the back and got ready ride out to the ring when the announcer called her name.

She was last, Erin had already gone. She'd performed the forward somersault perfectly, and looked like beauty in motion as she rode her horses around the ring, her limbs long and supple, her blonde hair flowing.

She hadn't seemed overly upset to see Blakely and Martin were now a couple. Maybe a bit of a turned up nose, but she wasn't brokenhearted, and Blakely didn't really feel bad for her.

Their rankings were on the board, and Erin was in first place.

As she sat on Candy's back at the tunnel entrance, she was able to pick out her parents in the stands, both of them standing and clapping as her name was called, along with her siblings and in-laws and nieces and nephews.

She was proud and pleased and felt loved and cared for, especially when she saw Martin down at the far end of the arena, sitting in the front row, leaning forward, his forearms on his knees, his eyes glued on her.

Just before she rode out she was able to pick out more people from her town, Mrs. Walter, Crew and Burgundy, Mrs. Gensimore and Mrs. Hutchison. People who loved her and cared about her and watched her grow up.

She thought of Erin, alone.

She had so much to be thankful for, so much that God had given her.

The idea that had been kind of rolling around in her head, that she would win the competition and then withdraw, staying home with Martin, making her life with him on his ranch, didn't seem like the best scenario anymore.

Oh, she still wanted to stay home. There was not a cell in her body that wanted to go out on the road with the trick show anymore. Not one.

But she thought, maybe winning the contest wasn't what she should be aiming for.

She had so much, and Erin had nothing.

Did she need to win the contest?

Would she be letting all of the people down who were here to see her if she didn't go out?

What if she didn't do her new trick? She could still give a great performance, doing everything perfectly, and come in second.

Part of her rebelled at that thought. Maybe it was pride. Probably was. She didn't want to come in behind Erin. She wanted to beat her, and then hand her the victory. Showing Erin that it was *her choice* to give the victory to her.

But that was arrogant and prideful, wasn't it?

None of her family knew about the new trick, no one from town.

Martin was the only one, and he'd understand when she explained to him later why she didn't do it.

With her mind made up, she gave Candy the signal, and they cantered out to the arena.

"I CAN'T BELIEVE you did that," Martin said, sitting on the ground, his back against a big rock, and Blakely cuddled between his legs. They were looking at the views from an overlook, one of many in the Ozark Mountains near Mistletoe and had just been talking about everything and anything. Taking a blissful day off work, the day after the competition.

"Actually, what I really can't believe, Whiplash," he said, "Is that you didn't tell me you were going to do that. You have no idea how worried I was when you finished up your routine in the arena and you hadn't done the new trick. I knew you wouldn't have chickened out, so I thought you must have gotten injured."

"I'm sorry. I didn't mean to worry you. But I told you, I realized that my pride was getting in the way of my love. And that was what I was struggling with. It wasn't about giving up, because it had become obvious that God had something better for me. But had it become about how much I loved others, and whether I loved them more than I love myself."

"That's deep." There was a little bit of tease in his voice, but she knew he was proud of her.

She laughed a little, as he'd intended. "Actually, it's simple. It's one of the simplest things that Jesus taught. But it's so hard to actually do."

"You can practice on me," Martin offered.

She giggled for the millionth time that day, and she wasn't a giggler. "You know I intend to."

He shifted, moving his arm from around her and taking out the box that he'd brought along with them before putting his arms back around her and opening it in front of her.

"Would you marry me? That would give you plenty of time to practice." His voice was lower and huskier, and he hadn't really meant it to be that way, but he was nervous, and he loved her. He wanted her to know.

He understood exactly what she was saying about putting others first.

"And, not that I want this to influence your answer, but you're the best person I know at putting others first, and I'm not only talking about what you did with Erin – about not doing what you knew you could, not needing to make yourself look better than her. Just so you know that. I don't think it's possible for me to be prouder of you than what I am."

Her head was shaking. He hoped that was not at his proposal. "If you only knew how many times I could see the opportunities to do things, and I turned away or ignored them because I'm too selfish. You wouldn't be proud at all."

"You can count those opportunities if you want to but don't feel guilty. Everyone does that. Everyone. But there aren't too many people who actually take any of those opportunities. I'm going to count the actual actions I see, and be proud. Now, are you trying to change the subject? Or was that a no?" He wiggled the box to remind her of the main subject.

"It's a yes." She turned her face to his, and kissed the side of his chin. "You know that. It's a good thing you asked me today, because if you hadn't of asked, I was gonna ask you. You're the whole reason I stayed home."

She meant it as a good thing, but it made his chest deflate. "I didn't want you to give all that up for me."

"I didn't want it anymore. I wanted you."

Her head turned back, and her finger came up and stroked the ring. "It's beautiful."

"I wasn't sure what you wanted, but I figured it was probably something simple. Something that wouldn't get in your way when we're working. If you don't like it we can get something else."

"This is perfect. I couldn't have picked out anything better." Her finger went from lightly touching the ring, to trailing along his hand and wrist. "I love that you know me so well. I love that you made that effort."

"Anything for you."

"I'm feeling the need to practice again."

"Funny. I was feeling that same need myself."

They both forgot about the ring as they shared a kiss that was so much better than the one that had won the kissing contest.

Epilogue

Race stared at the pizza in front of him.

"This is getting to be a thing for you," he said, his eyes twinkling at the woman he'd married twice sitting across the table from him.

"We should have had it with the children. Darcy and Frank would both have loved it."

"I'm sure they're eating plenty of junk food with Dante and Journee." He picked his pizza up, slowly, savoring it. This was a huge treat.

"Do you think they figured things out yet?" Penny asked, her own pizza held suspended in the air in front of her mouth.

"I don't think so." He narrowed his eyes, thinking back. And finally shaking his head. "No. I'm pretty sure not."

"Do you think it's going to work?" Penny asked, her brows lifted and a slight tinge of worry in her voice.

"I think so. We just need to give it some time. Journee isn't like the others."

"You're right. She's more in her head."

"Exactly. She needs to think about things, and she doesn't go jumping quite as quickly as, say, Blakely does." They shared a little smile. "She's not as contrary either."

"She's been hurt," Penny said, her face clouding, and her eyes pinching as though Journee's pain was her own.

"That's true." Race figured Penny probably did feel Journee's pain. It had hurt him to see her fall in love with a good man, a fairly good man, but one who wasn't strong enough to choose her over everything else. "It was a blessing it didn't work out, though. I think Journee sees that now."

"I think so. Any man who doesn't want her more than anyone else wouldn't have been a good choice. She wants someone who's going to love her above everyone. One whom she has no doubt about his love."

He nodded. "Because he won't have any doubt about hers."

Penny hadn't given him any specific glances, but guilt twisted Race's heart just the same. The first time they'd been married, everything else had come before her, and she'd finally not been able to take his neglect anymore and walked away.

He knew she regretted that decision, but he couldn't blame her for it. She'd been in a marriage by herself, and he had been married to his job. He couldn't believe she'd stayed as long as she had.

"I'm sorry."

She knew right away what he was talking about. "You don't have to apologize. Because you did that, I was able to tell Journee how blessed she was that she didn't get what she wanted. I know it probably didn't make her feel too much better at the time, but I know she appreciates it now. She knows that I was through it and that I know what I'm talking about at least."

"That doesn't keep me from regretting it though." He reached across the table and put his hand over top of hers. She twisted hers immediately and threaded their fingers together.

"What we have now is better than what we had then, now that

we've gone through the things we did. I know I'm grateful every day for what happened. Plus, we probably wouldn't have gotten the Barclay children."

"We might have ended up with kids of our own."

It felt bittersweet to him. Even though everything she said made sense, and he agreed with it all, and he knew that God had been in control of everything, and both of them were better people because of the pain they'd experienced in their first marriage. Still, he didn't like his part in it, and didn't want to ever go back to being the kind of person who only thought of himself, and neglected the people around him, the ones that were the most important to him, the ones who put up with him, and loved him despite all the things he wasn't, and never would be.

Penny being the chief of those.

"All things work together for good," Penny began.

"I know. It's still okay for me to have regrets though, isn't it? I don't want to forget. I don't want to brush it aside like it never happened, and I don't, under any circumstances, want it to happen again. I know you forgive me. I know God's forgiven me. And, I've forgiven myself, I think. But, I don't want it to just disappear. I need to remember, because for me to just shove it aside, and be happy that no one remembers or cares, might allow me to become complacent, and that's dangerous."

His wife knew exactly what he was talking about, although he probably didn't need her to understand. But he wanted her to know that he didn't think it was okay. And even though everything he had done was forgiven, he didn't want her to not get the credit she deserved for putting up with him, and then for giving him another chance.

"I'm glad we could get ourselves straightened out, because apparently our children needed us. I think we've done okay so far." Penny's pizza was gone, and she was looking at the box like she was contemplating a second piece.

"Just Journee left, and then Shawn. I don't know what we're going to do about Shawn."

"Journee's not in the bag yet, either."

"In the bag? I'm not sure she would appreciate us using that terminology."

"I'm pretty sure none of them would appreciate knowing what we had been up to. At least not until they'd fallen in love, and now I think they'd thank us. Journee's not quite there yet."

"You're right, my love, as usual." He sighed. "The letters worked to bring them together. And we were able to lure him to Mistletoe. But apparently neither one of them have given any identifying information in their letters."

"That was one of the rules for writing. To protect each party, because they were writing to strangers, they weren't allowed to give their personal information. At least we can be happy that both of them followed the rules."

"Yes but the rules are getting in the way now."

"I'm not sure that your congregation should hear you say that, Pastor," Penny said, emphasizing the word "pastor."

"You know what I meant. We made the rules, we can change them."

"I think they'll get this figured out. In fact, I've got a really good feeling about it. Do you want to bet a pizza?" she asked.

A grin spread over his face. "As a pastor, I can't bet." He looked at the box of pizza. "With anyone but my wife."

"I think you're making up your own rules," she said.

"I'm pretty sure the good Lord is okay with that. Between you and me." His thumb stroked over her hand, and he thought that maybe neither one of them would be having another piece of pizza.

Join Jessie's list and be the first to know about new releases and sales on her books!

Read Dreaming of His Pen Pal's Kiss, the next book in the Cowboy Mountain Christmas series where Journee finds out the identity of her pen pal and he's not what she thought! Keep reading for a sneak peek now.

Sneak Peek of Dreaming of His Pen Pal's Kiss

"Is that another name for your pen pal program?" Journee asked her dad while seated across the desk from him in his church office in Mistletoe, Arkansas.

"It is."

Her dad, glasses perched on the end of his nose, his salt-and-pepper hair not nearly as thick as it used to be, tapped the desk in front of him with one finger, as though thinking.

Journee's stomach shivered, just a little, for some odd reason. She already had four people she was writing to in the church's new pen pal program. But out of those four people, only one had written her more than once.

She wondered if she came on too strong in her original letter. Maybe she just didn't write the kind of letters people wanted to respond to. Maybe people were too busy. She didn't want to admit to her failure, but she had to admit to being discouraged.

Her dad, Pastor Race, tilted his head and narrowed his eyes just a little, as though he were thinking. Or as though he knew what she was going to say before she said it. Which was most likely the case.

Her mouth opened anyway, and the words he probably knew were going to come out spilled. "I can take the name."

"I haven't even told you whether it's a man or woman." Humor laced his words, along with a heavy dose of affection.

She'd lost her parents when she was pretty young, and it was funny how she had nothing but good memories of them. Like her brain had completely blanked out and recorded over anything bad that had ever happened.

Still, Race and Penny had adopted her and her five siblings, and she honestly had nothing but good memories of them either. It wasn't that everything that had ever happened in her life had been good, other than her parents being killed a car accident, but God had blessed her with two sets of wonderful parents.

She wasn't quite sure why, when some people didn't even get one.

"Dad, you know it doesn't matter. I just love writing people. Or maybe, I just love writing in general. And things really get slow in the ER at night. I have plenty of time."

The ER in a small town was an odd thing. For days, they'd go with barely a soul showing up, and then one night, they might have nothing but chaos all night long.

Most of the time though, it was quiet and she had plenty of time to daydream or, as she'd been doing, write her letters.

"I know you do. I just don't want to give you more than you can handle." He tapped his finger some more. "Although, while I do have at least forty people writing from the church, I have more requests for partners than I do people to match them with. I was almost thinking of writing to this person myself."

Whoever it was, they would definitely benefit from writing to her dad more than they would from writing to her. She'd never met a wiser person.

"Maybe that's what the Lord would want you to do."

Race shook his head slightly. "Actually, when the name first came in, I thought of you immediately. I probably would have asked you to do it then if I didn't know you were already paired up with four people."

"Dad, I can do it. Especially if you think I should. If you think it's meant for me." She tried to keep the hope out of her voice. All of her siblings except Shawn, who would probably never get married, had found God's plan for them and, at the same time, found a lifetime love.

It was her fondest hope.

She thought she'd had it with her high school sweetheart.

Thoughts of Alex turned the excited shiver in her stomach into something which felt more like congealed gravy.

Thoughts of Alex didn't hurt anymore, but they made her sad.

Because she viewed him as a big mistake.

And wished she wouldn't have wasted so much time on him when she was younger. Maybe she'd missed God's plan and God's big love story for her because she'd been focused on the wrong guy— because she'd definitely been focused on Alex.

Or maybe Alex had been right for her, and he just hadn't been strong enough to stand up to his parents and say so.

But she didn't want a man who wasn't respectful to his parents, and she admired him in an odd kind of way for listening to them.

Still, it was hard not to think of what might have been.

Her dad didn't answer for a moment, and she gave him time. He'd warned her from the beginning that Alex probably wasn't right for her. Not in so many words, but anytime she'd gone to him for advice, his advice would have turned her away from Alex.

To her shame, she hadn't usually listened and hadn't gone to him as much as she probably should have anyway.

Her dad breathed deeply and straightened the pen in front of him that was already straight before looking up at her. "This was a little different. And I think there's potential on both ends for things to go badly, so while I know that you have never had a problem obeying the rules, I'm going to remind you. It is imperative that you not use your real name and that you not ask for theirs."

She nodded. She'd not broken any of the pen pal program's rules, and she didn't plan to.

"It's also important that you don't give too many identifying details about your life."

He smiled, the love he felt for her reaching deep inside and swirling around her chest. From the very beginning, she'd never had a doubt about how Race and Penny felt about her. It was amazing that they loved her no matter how stupid she was. How many dumb mistakes she made. And how often she messed up and didn't listen.

After the debacle with Alex, she couldn't imagine her dad giving her advice that she didn't follow.

"I suppose I'm a little overprotective of you, because not only are you my daughter, but you're the youngest. I know you're all grown up now, able to support yourself, and you don't need your old dad anymore..."

"I need you, Dad. Don't ever say that I don't. I would have avoided a lot of heartache in my life if I would have listened to you."

"Water under the bridge." He shook his head and reached his hand out across the desk. She put hers in it easily. Race and Penny had never hesitated to hug them or touch them, and she appreciated it. It was part of what made her feel loved.

"Regardless. Your advice means everything to me. Whatever you say, I'll do it to the best of my ability."

"Thank you. I know you will. You were such an easy child to raise. And you've grown into such a wonderful woman. But I don't want to see you hurt. And..." He looked down at the name in front of him. "I think this person is vulnerable too. I know you would never do anything to harm them on purpose, and I don't think that most people would look at this person and see how fragile they are, but I just want you both to be careful. At least for a year. If you're still writing after that time, I think it would be safe to say you could probably open up a little more."

He said the last slowly, like he hadn't quite thought it through. His eyes were on the calendar, and Journee's eyes landed there too.

February seventh.

The rest of the world would be celebrating Valentine's Day tomorrow, but not in Mistletoe, Arkansas. For them, it was Christmas year-round.

"I don't have a problem with that, Dad. No identifying details, and no names, and no real address, until we've been writing for a year."

She looked down, running her finger over the picture frame on her dad's desk that held the first picture of their family that had ever been taken. Race and Penny stood behind them with Ethan, whom they'd never adopted but had lived with them for a while, with Journee and her five siblings in front.

A hodgepodge of people maybe, but she loved that picture, because it represented a new beginning. She thought her birth parents would smile at where their children had landed and what God had done for them.

Still, Race hesitated, and she felt she needed to say something. "Dad, if you don't think that this is something I should do, don't give it to me."

He was silent for a bit, although the air around them was alive. Sounds of children from the daycare playing on the playground outside came muffled through the window, and ladies' laughter from the Bible study down the hall seemed to seep under the door.

That was one of her favorite things about the church. She could go into the sanctuary and just feel the stillness and peace of God, and she could walk out of the sanctuary and feel the life and breath of the saints who made up the church.

It was just a building, but it always felt alive to her. Always gave her peace. Comfort. And hope.

Finally, Race shifted and swallowed. "No. I actually know this is something you should do." Concern overshadowed every other emotion on his face. "I want to protect you. I know your heart was already broken, and love can be hard sometimes. Not that I'm expecting you to fall in love with this person."

He tapped the paper on the desk. "Not romantic love. But even friends can break your heart. I just can't help but think that even though I know this is what you're supposed to do, there's going to be tears ahead. As a father, I don't want that. Still, I know that sometimes it's the hard times in our life where we grow the most. It's what God uses to bring us closer to Him and to make us into the people that he wants us to be. I can definitely look back over my own life and see that as a stark reality. The hardest times of my life ended up being the best times for me. It's just...they're so hard to walk through. But I think even more than that, it's hard to watch people we love walk through them. If you love someone, their pain is yours. So, if I'm hesitating, maybe it's about my own heart as much as it's about yours."

Journee smiled at that. Her dad wasn't more concerned about himself than her, but he was also a humble man, and he wouldn't boast. "I love that you care about me. And I know I am a dreamer. I know I have a tendency to make really bad decisions, but I think I'm doing better, and I'm also stronger than what I get credit for. I might be the youngest, but I am grown up."

She didn't really mind the tendency of everyone in her family to treat her like she was still a child. In some ways, she kinda felt like she was.

She had made some foolish choices. Although, at least for the way some people thought, she'd made a wise decision in completing her four-year nursing degree, but she'd passed up a lot more lucrative opportunities in order to come back to her hometown and settle down. She had no desire to leave her family and friends in the town she grew up in.

None.

"I know you do."

At that, Race pushed back away from the desk and came around. Journee stood, and he embraced her, the strength of his arms and the scent of his aftershave familiar and beloved, comforting, making her feel safe like she always did when Race hugged her. She knew he'd protect her with everything he had, but she also knew she was an adult and had to be responsible for her own decisions and her own life.

He squeezed her for a bit and pulled away first. "Here's the address. It's a man. He's not retired. And, like all of the other pen pal recipients in our program, he's in the hospital. He hasn't been in quite as long as most of the others, only a couple of weeks, but because of the nature of his job, people who care about him know that being in the hospital is psychologically excruciating for him. They felt that giving him a pen pal—someone like you," Race said with a smile, "is what he needs to get himself back to where he needs to be in order to do his job to the best of his ability."

"Are you saying he's depressed?" She tilted her head, having had some experience with depression in her schooling. Also, Alex had been going to be a psychologist.

"I don't think he's there. Yet. I do think it's a distinct possibility, especially if he doesn't get better." Race's words were slightly hesitant, like he didn't want to say too much.

Journee nodded. She didn't need to know all the details. She had a good imagination, and she could fill them in with whatever she wanted. She could have a conversation with herself. Or with a reluctant man who needed to be encouraged. Of course, she had been worried she came on too strong with her other pen pals. Maybe she should start slowly.

"I'll do my best, Dad."

"I knew you would, Journee. I love you." He squeezed her again before letting go.

She fingered the paper as she walked out of his office. Somehow, the idea of this pen pal, and writing to this man, stirred threads of excitement that she hadn't had when her dad had handed her the addresses to the other people.

She had a feeling...this man was going to be different.

Sign up for Jessie's newsletter! Get a free book, access to exclusive bonus content, get fun and funny updates on her life on the farm and more!

A Gift from Jessie

View this code through your smart phone camera to be taken to a page where you can download a FREE ebook when you sign up to get updates from Jessie Gussman! Find out why people say, "Jessie's is the only newsletter I open and read" and "You make my day brighter. Love, love, love reading your newsletters. I don't know where you find time to write books. You are so busy living life. A true blessing." and "I know from now on that I can't be drinking my morning coffee while reading your newsletter – I laughed so hard I sprayed it out all over the table!"

Claim your free book from Jessie!

Escape to more faith-filled romance series by Jessie Gussman!

The Complete Sweet Water, North Dakota Reading Order:

Series One: Sweet Water Ranch Western Cowboy Romance (11 book series)

Series Two: Coming Home to North Dakota (12 book series)

Series Three: Flyboys of Sweet Briar Ranch in North Dakota (13 book series)

Series Four: Sweet View Ranch Western Cowboy Romance (10 book series)

Spinoffs and More! Additional Series You'll Love:

Jessie's First Series: Sweet Haven Farm (4 book series)

Small-Town Romance: The Baxter Boys (5 book series)

Bad-Boy Sweet Romance: Richmond Rebels Sweet Romance (3 book series)

Sweet Water Spinoff: Cowboy Crossing (9 book series)

Small Town Romantic Comedy: Good Grief, Idaho (5 book series)

True Stories from Jessie's Farm: Stories from Jessie Gussman's Newsletter (3 book series)

Reader-Favorite! Sweet Beach Romance: Blueberry Beach (8 book series)

Blueberry Beach Spinoff: Strawberry Sands (10 book series)

From Strawberry Sands to: Raspberry Ridge (12 book series)

Swoonfully Jolly Holiday Stories:

Holiday Romance: Cowboy Mountain Christmas (6 book series)

Cowboy Mountain Christmas Spinoff: A Heartland Cowboy Christmas (9 book series)

New and Much Loved: Mistletoe Meadows (4 books and counting!)

Laughing Through the Snow: Christmas Tree, PA Sweet Romcoms (6 short reads)

www.ingramcontent.com/pod-product-compliance
Lightning Source LLC
Chambersburg PA
CBHW031048310726
48969CB00007B/2178